BEDSIDE MANNERS

For Physicians and Everybody Else

WHAT THEY DON'T TEACH
IN MEDICAL SCHOOL
(OR ANY OTHER SCHOOL)

Scott Abramson M.D.

ISBN 978-1-68526-379-9 (Paperback)
ISBN 978-1-68526-380-5 (Digital)

Covenant Books
11661 Hwy 707
Murrells Inlet, SC 29576
www.covenantbooks.com

CONTENTS

ACKNOWLEDGMENTS

There are so many people who have made this book possible. They have made it possible because they have made *me* possible. These are some of them:

Dr. Terry Stein, who first encouraged me to write monthly communication articles for my Kaiser Permanente colleagues, and who, along with Dr. Bob Tull and later Cecilia Runkle, championed the communication mission at Kaiser Permanente Northern California.

Executive leaders of the ten-thousand-physician-strong Northern California Kaiser Permanente Medical Group, especially former CEO Dr. Robert Pearl under whose leadership, the mission of physician communication was envisioned and then enthusiastically supported, as well as current CEO Dr. Richard Isaacs under whose leadership the mission continues to flourish.

Kaiser Permanente Northern California regional leaders of the Communication Committee and Physician Health and Wellness Committee, whose inspiration and guidance were essential to the success of this mission: Dr. John Chuck, Dr. Denise Brahan, Rae Oser, and Leslie Koved, to name a few.

Physician leaders at my local Kaiser hospital (San Leandro-Fremont) who have given our committees the freedom to develop programs from the ground up. In particular—Dr. Barry Scurran, Dr. Calvin Wheeler, Dr. Rob Greenberg, Dr. Suhani Mody (may her soul rest in peace), and our current physician leaders Dr. Kapil Dhingra and Dr. Eric Cain.

Dr. Rochelle Frank, a former Kaiser colleague and now professor at California Northstate Medical School, who, in my retirement, has graciously kept me in the communication mission, working as volunteer faculty with medical students in that school.

My Toastmasters muse, Sharon Luther, who inspired several stories in this book.

My colleagues on our local Kaiser hospital (San Leandro-Fremont), Physician Communication Committee, and the Physician Health and Wellness Committee. Working together not only brought beneficial programs to our physician colleagues but also brought our committee teams a joyous comradery.

In this regard, let me specifically mention Dr Jennifer Teng, chair of our local Physician Communication Committee, and Dr. Vallari Shukla, my partner as cochair for many years on the Physician Health and Wellness Committee. Finally, my "brother" and my personal "bullsh——t detector," Dr. Alan Jung, whose commonsense wisdom kept me grounded in all these endeavors.

My colleagues and staff in the Neurology Department at Kaiser Permanente Hayward–San Leandro: Dr. Allan Bernstein, who in 1979 took the risk and hired me to begin my Kaiser Permanente career; Dr. Will North, my colleague in our Neurology Department, whose door was always open to my bitching and moaning; and Robyn Reince, head nurse of Neurology Department (my personal Radar O'Reilly), who often knew what I was thinking and what I needed before I'd know them myself.

Susan Garcia, my former medical assistant, who has more common sense than 99 percent of all physicians I have known, including myself.

Aileen Ross (may her soul rest in peace), our EEG technician who, for over forty years, did not only take electrical readings of our patients' brain waves but also listened to their stories and offered them the healings of a woman imbued with love and with faith.

All my Kaiser physician colleagues, nurses, and support staff who have made my forty-year career such a blessing. Let me salute you with a heartfelt remembrance of a Kaiser Permanente advertising slogan of yesteryear: "Good People. Good Medicine."

The great teachers in my life: Miss Margaret Dean, my fifth- and sixth-grade teacher at Morningside Elementary School, who encouraged me never to accept mediocrity, Rabbi Nat Ezray, who not only taught the wisdom of Torah but also role-modeled the art of teaching; Dr. Mahendra Somasundaran, my attending neurologist at Kings County Hospital, Brooklyn, New York, who has been the role model of the physician I hoped to become; and Dennis Prager whose wisdom has guided my life in meaningful ways.

Our spiritual leaders, Rabbi Corey Helfand, who made me "want to be a better man" (see the essay on leadership), and Cantor Doron Shapira, who for so many years has been the backbone of our Peninsula Sinai Congregation in Foster City, California.

My personal therapists over the years who helped maintain what sanity I have had: Dr. Anne Paley, who, after six years of therapy in my resident training years, gave me the best counsel I ever got—"Scott," she advised. "Be kind to yourself."—and Dr. Robert Lieb, who is currently helping me to fulfill Dr. Paley's advice.

My parents, George and Esther Abramson, who were married for over seventy years and whose love of learning was only exceeded by their love for each other.

My family, my two sons Jonathan and Jeremy, who have taught me, and continue to teach me, the humbling lessons of parenthood.

And lastly my wife, Pamela, who has stood by my side and the side of our family during my forty-year Kaiser career, through the missed dinners, the nights interrupted by 2:00 a.m. phone calls, the weekends spent in the hospital, and the vacations partly stolen by my Kaiser hospital laptop that obsessively called me to its service. Pamela, we have shared the highs, the lows, and the in-betweens of forty-four years of marriage and over forty years of my Kaiser Permanente physician career. You were always there. Thank you, my darling.

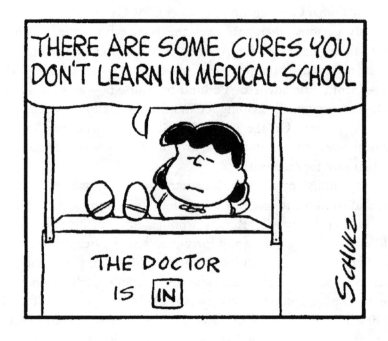

INTRODUCTION

STORY NO. 1

Having had referred Rose for a minor surgical procedure a few months previously, this very sweet eighty-three-year-old square dance instructor was now on my schedule for a return visit. Since I had heard of no complications, I figured things went pretty well in the surgery. And since I was running late that day, I was hoping this return visit would be a quick and easy one:

"Feeling great now, Dr. Abramson...thanks for arranging the surgery... Bye-bye now." Who knows? If I got lucky, maybe Rose might even bake me some little old lady brownies.

Therefore, when Rose informed me that, in fact, she did not undergo the recommended surgery, I was a little surprised.

"I would not let that surgeon touch me with a ten-foot laser beam," was the way Rose explained it. And what she said next gave me a jolt. I guess it was the mismatch of the picture: this sweet lady in her gardening bonnet (she and her husband refer to each other as "mama" and "papa") and the words she spoke next.

"That surgeon you sent me to, Dr. Abramson," she declared, "is one pompous little prick!"

And you know the funny thing is...she was right.

I know him. He is a technical whiz. A brilliant surgeon.

But Rose nailed it.

Personality wise, he is, well, kind of what Rose said.

Commentary Story No. 1

Consider this:

What good did the brilliance of this surgeon do for him? What good were his finely trained technical skills? He could not help his patient. And he couldn't help, not because he lacked the skill to help but because he lacked the ability to communicate that he had the skills to help.

He couldn't help because he could not close the deal. He could not make the sale. And let's face it...we are all salesmen. We're all selling something.

Maybe it's a product.

Maybe it's a service.

Maybe it's an idea.

And as physicians and healers, what we're selling is *trust*.

Trust in...

Our competence.

Our compassion.

Our character.

And if we can't sell that, will our patients pick up the blood pressure medications we prescribe or the colonoscopy we recommend?

What good will become of our training, our knowledge, our expertise?

To tell the truth, as a physician, I am honored to be called a salesman.

I just hope I have been, and will continue to be, a good one.

STORY NO. 2

My colleague, Marcia, is a busy internal medicine physician. She is also a wife and a mom. And like most of us, Marcia, too, struggles with work-life balance. The children in her daughter's second-grade class made Mother's Day cards. Her daughter very proudly brought home the card she had made. Marcia's daughter gave it to the nanny.

Commentary Story No. 2

It's tough being a physician.
It may be even tougher being a woman physician.
Work-life balance, resilience, and combatting burnout is a challenge not just among physicians but for everyone.

STORY NO. 3

Wayne has been a longtime patient in my neurology clinic. He has multiple sclerosis. The disease took its inexorable toll. He had become wheelchair-bound. He could no longer work as a maintenance mechanic. His wife had to go back to work to support their three sons. Things were tough for Wayne and his family. His wife was worn-out with her three-hours-daily commute and full-time job. Wayne tried to help out in the house by doing dishes, ironing, and cleaning, but it was difficult for him. His wife (and Wayne fully acknowledges she was justified) often came home frazzled and took out her irritation on him. In Wayne's eyes, his three sons seemed to no longer look upon him as a father, but more as a family burden.

Nowadays his mother brought him to his neurology clinic appointments. She told me Wayne, growing up, was the comedian of the family. His two older siblings would often pound him down in their brotherly fights. Mom convinced Wayne at an early age to fight back, not with his fists, but with humor. So when his bigger brothers would get ready to punch out his lights, Wayne would grin and dramatically plead, "Please, Bossman, please, Bossman, don't hit me!"

His brothers would roar with laughter; Wayne got spared a brotherly beating.

As we ended the visit, in spite of everything, it seemed Wayne's old sense of humor had never left him.

"One great thing about being in a wheelchair," Wayne smiled, "is that your shoes never wear out."

Commentary Story No. 3

Every day I try to remember those words.
Every day I try to be grateful that my own shoes…do wear out.

For over forty years, I have been a physician. Now retired, I was a neurologist at Kaiser Permanente Medical Group in Northern California. During that time, I was privileged to serve as one of the leaders in Kaiser's Physician Communication mission (teaching "bedside manners" to our doctors) and as one of the leaders in Physician Wellness mission (teaching resilience to our doctors).

For the last twenty years of my medical career, I told a story every month on these topics (physician communication and physician resilience) for the ten thousand physicians in our Kaiser Permanente Northern California Medical Group. During these years, I was also blessed to have heard so many inspiring stories from my colleagues and from my patients. What follows were some of these stories. While these stories were birthed from my forty-year career in medicine, I believe their lessons could be helpful to folks in all walks of life.

I myself struggled with these issues of communication, resilience, and even burnout. Some of the stories you will read are not pleasant ones for me to tell. I am not proud of some of the things they reveal about me, both professionally and personally. But that is one of the reasons I write them: I believe the vulnerabilities and insecurities I expose about myself are common to many physicians and, in fact, to almost every one of the human persuasion. My hope is that by acknowledging those painful vulnerabilities and insecurities within one's own persona, it can lead to understanding and to kindness toward oneself. And I hope some of the people who you will meet in these stories, by their grit and by their grace, may bring inspiration to you as they have to me.

BEDSIDE MANNERS— THE UGLY

"DO YOU REALLY NEED THIS APPOINTMENT?"

Dawn called me in my neurology clinic for an appointment. Her story was a sad one. At age thirty-five, this once-vibrant executive secretary and devoted single mom was struck down with multiple sclerosis. Over the past two years, the disease had ravaged her nervous system. She was now wheelchair-bound. She needed help dressing, bathing, and even feeding herself. Her mother, who had moved in to be her caregiver, was now changing her diapers (once again).

I will be honest. I did not want to see Dawn. I knew there was nothing I could do. At her past visits, I had asked my routine neurological questions. I had performed my perfunctory neurological examination. I had felt helpless. The thought of seeing her in person again, frankly, saddened me.

So I had my nurse call Dawn with these questions (hopefully to avoid the face-to-face visit I did not relish):

Was there any change in her condition? Dawn answered, "No."

Did she have any specific concerns? Dawn answered, "No."

Could we handle this appointment by phone? Dawn answered, "No."

Did she think this in-person appointment was necessary? Dawn answered, "Yes."

Dawn and her mother came in for the appointment. There was nothing new. There was no change in her condition. I asked my routine medical questions. I did my perfunctory neurological exam. And again, as in previous encounters, I felt helpless.

2

Yet strangely enough, Dawn and her mom seemed satisfied with the appointment. An appointment, frankly, I had considered a waste of my doctor-time.

Upon leaving Dawn turned to me and smiled. "We knew there was nothing you could do for me, Dr. Abramson. We just wanted to hear your voice."

The power of our presence.

No matter who we are or what we do for a living, it still matters.

Too bad we physicians and healers sometimes forget.

Mea culpa.

DO THESE WORDS OF REASSURANCE WORK?

Years ago, my friend Michael was having an unusual headache. He thought it was some sort of migraine. His wife, Barbara, took him to a local emergency room. Upon full evaluation in ER it turned out this was far more serious. It was metastatic brain cancer from a newly discovered lung tumor. Michael was thirty-five years old, ate healthy, never smoked, and jogged five miles every day. He and Barbara had two young sons. Upon hearing the news, Barbara was devastated beyond description. A doctor came in, took her aside, and said these words:

"Don't worry," he reassured her. "you're a strong woman. You'll be able to raise those two boys on your own."

Michael died within a year.

Barbara, now twenty years later, has survived her grief.

But she has never forgiven that doctor for his phony words of reassurance.

BEDSIDE MANNERS—THE BAD

TOMMY'S TOE

Tommy tried to kick his sister's teddy bear across the room, but he missed and kicked a cabinet instead. His fourth toe was purple, swollen, and very tender. His mom brought him to a nearby minor injury clinic.

Tommy said they sent him for pictures, and then he saw the doctor. The doctor looked at the pictures and then looked at his toe. Then he told Tommy to move his foot. The doctor said the X-ray pictures looked okay. Nothing was busted. Then the doctor told Tommy and his mom they could go home.

The toe healed just fine. Tommy was back to kicking his sister's teddy bears. But Tommy thought the doctor wasn't very good. He thought the doctor wasn't very good because he didn't even touch the sore toe. Even an eight-year-old kid knows what happens when you visit the doctor. They're supposed to touch the boo-boo.

Maybe Hippocrates was right.

"The physician must be experienced in many things," he said, "but most assuredly in touching."

"I WILL HAVE TO ASK THE CHEF!"

At the Foster City IHOP, I ordered three egg Western omelet breakfast. I gave the waiter my usual specifics:

- Substitute cheddar cheese for jack.
- Make hash browns well-done.
- Replace toast with English muffin.
- Hold the ham.

The waiter dutifully took down my order. As he was about to leave, I added my final request.

"Would it be possible," I asked, "to make the omelet with eggbeaters?"

Rolling his eyes just enough for me to notice and sighing with an unmistaken annoyed edge to his voice, the waiter announced, "I will have to ask the chef."

He snapped his order pad closed, turned smartly, and made his exit.

Now here I am, valued IHOP customer, and suddenly I felt small. I felt disrespected. And I felt resentful toward my waiter.

So what had this got to do with us physician healers?

Consider this: When our valued "customers" ask that one final question, when they make that one last "one foot out the door" request, how often can they detect in our tone of voice, "I will have to ask the chef."?

Addendum: I just can't wait till IHOP mails me their waiter evaluation survey.

7

BEDSIDE MANNERS—THE GOOD

WHAT SIZE LEECH?
WE CAN PERHAPS PROMISE OUR
PATIENTS SOMETHING MORE
IMPORTANT THAN A CURE

In June 2003 my father suffered a stroke. He could not speak. A speech therapist named Pam Brown came to our home. Pam Brown was wonderful. She was filled determination and hope. After she completed her evaluation, she hugged my mother and then she hugged me. When Pam gave me that goodbye hug, I could not help it. I began to cry. Now Pam probably thought my tears were for Dad. But I knew that wasn't it. Dad was 101 years old. His life had been rich and full. It wasn't that.

The reason I cried was because of what Pam said just before she left.

"Scott," she said, "I cannot promise you success. I cannot promise your dad will speak again. But I will promise you this: In the month I have been given to work with your dad, I will do my flat-out best. I will give everything I have. I will not let up. That I will promise. I give you my word."

What a powerful way to connect with our patients! Pam Brown did not promise a cure, nor did she promise success. What she did promise was a pledge of personal commitment.

At that moment, I felt so connected, so bonded to speech therapist Pam Brown that had Pam recommended bloodletting... I would have simply asked, "Pam Brown, what size leech?"

HOW A MOTORCYCLE HELMET CAN IMPROVE COMMUNICATION WITH OUR PATIENTS

One of the techniques taught in our Kaiser Permanente communication model was to engage each of our patients by making some sort of social comment.

Something like…

"Gee whiz, Ms. Jones, can you believe this weather?" or "Yeah, Dwayne, how 'bout them Raiders!"

Though it may be a minor thing, such "break the ice" social comments could build connection with our patients.

But many of us in the health care field found trying to make this social chitchat, well, kind of a stretch.

By nature we may be shy and reserved.

Small talk may not come easy for us.

Many of us, I suspect, are not the life of the cocktail party.

A single friend of mine, a self-described dweeb, once lamented to me that he could never "score with the hot chicks." (His words, not mine.) He explained he had always been shy around girls. He was "small-talk challenged." He said he never knew how to start a conversation with those of the female persuasion. Then he had an epiphany. Although he knew nothing about motorcycles, in fact, would have been terrified to ride one, he bought himself a motorcycle helmet. Then flaunting this piece of equipment, he swaggered into the coolest singles bar around.

To his amazement, he was now surrounded by "hot chicks" eagerly seeking his companionship.

So what's the point?

For those of us physicians and healers who are small-talk challenged, why not try on our own "motorcycle helmets"? As we engage our patients in this bit of social conversation, why not try shifting the focus of that conversation to us? I know one doctor who has a picture of his beloved golden retriever, Max, on his exam room wall, and yet another whose wall is decorated with photos of her Hawaiian vacation. Another doctor wears ties emblazoned with Looney Tunes characters. He tells me he has had some great conversations with his patients about the Road Runner and Daffy Duck.

All these things can easily get a little social conversation going. That conversation can build connection, that connection can build trust, and that trust can enhance compliance. And if patients follow our advice, hopefully they will achieve better health.

And it's so easy!

Instead of struggling with our clumsy attempts to make small talk about the weather or Raider football, let's allow ourselves to become the topic of the conversation.

So whether we are riding a Harley, strutting into a hot singles bar, or making doctor chitchat with our patients, here's a tip: "Wear your helmet!"

HOW A LITTLE SELF-REVELATION CAN BUILD PATIENT TRUST

Fred and Doris came to my neurology clinic for consultation. Fred had Alzheimer's disease. Doris, his devoted caregiver wife of fifty-seven years' marriage, was filled with take-charge energy and the latest literature from AARP.

Now here were my assumptions about the visit:

Doris knew she was seeing the specialist. (That would be me.)

She heard with her own ears my expert history-taking questions.

She witnessed my superb physical examination skills.

She was awed (or at least should have been) as I answered her questions with brilliance.

All in all I'm thinking Doris must have been pretty darn impressed with (and grateful to have seen) this particular neurology specialist.

But as Doris was leaving, something happened that made me realize I had not really impressed her all that much. In fact, I had not even come close to gaining her confidence and her trust.

Escorting her and Fred out the door, I mentioned that my own father, too, had Alzheimer's disease. Doris turned to me, her eyes softening as she grasped my hand between hers.

"Oh, Doctor," she smiled almost tearfully, "so you do understand."

It's funny.

The expert history inquiry.

The superb neurological examination.

The brilliant explanations.

All meant zilch until we connected by a personal revelation.

"YOU MATTER"

After admitting a sick child to the hospital ICU, my colleague spoke with the worried mom and dad in the waiting room. A short time later, as he went off hospital call, he brought the oncoming pediatric hospital doctor to meet the parents. When they both entered the waiting room, not only were Mom and Dad waiting, but there were about twenty-nine other folks present: uncles, aunts, friends, the pastor, the deacons, and the Prayer Sisters of the Church. For the next three minutes, the new doctor calmly went to each person, introduced herself, and then patiently asked each their own name.

Yes, I realize this action did take a few precious minutes of time. I get that. But think about the message. To everyone in that room, the message was simply this: "Not only does your child matter, but *you* matter."

Bumper sticker seen by me a while ago: "Be Somebody who makes Everybody feel like Somebody."

Okay. This is one of those tacky, feel-good, Hallmark-card, bumper-sticker platitudes that sound so cool that we then forget five seconds later. But I bet on that night, in that hospital ICU pediatric waiting room, there were twenty-nine worried people who will never forget a doctor who made them feel like "somebody."

AN EXTRAORDINARY WAY TO CONNECT WITH OUR PATIENTS

I had a minor skin problem. I saw my dermatologist. On that visit, I learned from her an extraordinary way to connect with patients, something I myself had not practiced much and, truth be told, was not too good at either. As Dr. Eunice Tsai entered the exam room, she greeted me with a warm, glorious, sparkling, radiant, and welcoming smile. In that moment, not one word was spoken. And in that moment, I felt wonderfully bonded with my doctor. And because of that instant bond, I knew I would be perfectly willing to follow whatever dermatological recommendations she had in mind. Had Dr. Tsai then advised I cover my skin with peanut butter, I would have simply asked, "Smooth or crunchy, Doc?"

But it reminded me that this smiling business was something that was not part of my routine medical practice. Oh sure, as I greet my patients, I may attempt a polite, professional pseudo-grin. But a glorious, sparkling, radiant, warm, and welcoming smile?

Nope.

Not me.

I guess I'm just one of those who are "radiant-smile challenged."

Sometimes, a smile, the simplest of human expressions, can become most profoundly meaningful.

Sometimes it can become an extraordinary way to connect with other humans, especially those who come to us for healing.

Addendum: Lately I've made a smile commitment. Nowadays, at least once with every patient, I actually try to smile. I got some good feedback too. One of my long-term patients, a very nice elderly woman whom I had known for years, remarked, "Dr. Abramson, you have such a nice smile."

Then she added, "I did not even know you had teeth!"

BEDSIDE MANNERS—THE APOLOGY

"THAT DOCTOR DID NOT EVEN HAVE THE COMMON DECENCY TO..."

My son's middle-school principal had a very negative medical experience. On a scheduled appointment, a doctor kept him waiting over forty-five minutes.

"I understand that doctors are busy. I know that they have emergencies and can run late," the principal told me. "But what really got me was that the doctor did not even have the common decency to make an apology!"

Not that I personally would ever run behind schedule or keep my patients waiting (ha ha), but apologizing for keeping someone waiting forty-five minutes seemed just good manners. Yet many times it seems we physicians are unable to take two seconds to utter the words "I'm late. I apologize." And while our patients realize we may not be able to always be on time, like my son's middle-school principal, they do expect from us the common decency to make an apology.

Just one concluding thought.

In the memorable words of Ali McGraw, the heroine in the movie *Love Story*, if being in love means "*never* having to say you're sorry," then as physicians and healers, being late should mean "*always* having to say you're sorry."

But then again (in the words of Tina Turner), "What's love got to do with it?"

We're talkin' about common decency.

"YOU HAD ME AT..."

A few months ago, I had the opportunity to speak with my personal customer service representative at AT&T. I had had an issue with my phone bill. After navigating through the prerequisite twenty-three levels of phone mail hell, I finally got to speak with someone of the human persuasion. She was very nice. She solved my problem. But before she hung up, I felt duty bound to give her and her organization a much-needed mini seminar on efficient business practices.

"I know it's not your fault personally," I began, "but it is unacceptable to keep your customers waiting on the phone for nineteen minutes and twenty-nine seconds."

She listened patiently to my tale of voice mail woe and to my tips on customer service.

"Mr. Abramson," she responded, "I am sorry."

Impressed by her sincerity and her compassion, almost instantly, my internal grumpy meter fell back into the "peace and love" zone (where it usually resides). Anyway I felt calmed. My complaint was acknowledged, and my frustration was assuaged. But then she blew it. What she said next nullified all the good she had just done.

"You see, Mr. Abramson," she explained, "our Bakersfield phone bank has had staffing problems all day. In addition, our main West Coast server has had a momentary power outage, and of course, calls are especially heavy in this 2 p.m. to 5 p.m. time slot. Perhaps in the future, for faster service, you'd like to handle this on our internet website. It's www..."

It was too bad. She almost pulled it off. But I didn't need to hear about phone bank staffing problems, computer glitches, or internet options. I didn't need to hear these detailed excuses. She had me at "I'm sorry."

Here's the point:

- People don't care why we're late.
- People don't need an explanation.
- People don't want an explanation.
- All they want is a simple apology.

Not everything works right all the time in our medical organizations. Sometimes things go wrong. Sometimes our customers have a right to be cranky. And when things do go wrong, we all try to make the appropriate apologies to our patients. But I wonder how many times these apologies turn into long-winded excuses. I wonder how many times our patients might be shaking their heads at us, thinking, *Gee whiz, you had me at "I'm sorry."*

ONE THING YOUR COMPUTER WILL NEVER DO

At the start of every patient visit, Dr. Todd Weitzenberg, my colleague at Santa Rosa, says he makes an apology to his patients.

"I want to apologize to you personally, Ms. Jones," Todd begins, "for the attention I will be giving to my computer during our time together. You may see me madly typing away. I may not be making much eye contact. It may seem like I'm ignoring you. I want to apologize right now for all that. But here's the good stuff..." (and then Todd shows the benefits of computer technology, like having X-rays at one's fingertips, expediting prescriptions to the pharmacy, etc.).

"And best of all, Ms. Jones," Todd concludes, "after I type the report of your visit, other doctors will actually be able to read my handwriting!"

Now imagine being one of Todd's patients. Perhaps you were feeling a little snubbed playing second fiddle to a fifteen-inched flat screen. Wouldn't such an apology make you feel just a little less neglected?

Computers and computerized medicine can do wonderful things for our practice. But let's not forget that what we do is still about that sacred connection between one human physician and one human patient. Making an apology for our computer is one way to honor that sacred connection.

And come to think of it, maybe that's one thing that separates us humans from our computer counterparts.

When has a computer apologized to anyone?

For anything?

Ever?

BEDSIDE MANNERS—SAYING "NO"

ADVICE ON MUD WRESTLING
HOW TO SAY "NO" AND
FEEL GOOD ABOUT IT

Lottie Wilson, four feet and eleven inches of no-nonsense grit, was the toughest teacher I ever had in my high school years at Georgia Military Academy. Miss Lottie never argued with her students about the Algebra grades she gave us or the homework we claimed we lost on the school bus. "When you mud wrestle with a pig," Miss Lottie said, "you both get dirty...but only the pig enjoys it."

We all have those challenging, "unlucky" patients (customers), who are so "unlucky" that shortly after we prescribe them their Percocet tablets, doggone it, their purses get stolen! Go figure. And although we sometimes end up mud wrestling with them about why Bowser keeps chewing up the Percocet, we, healers, I suspect, just like Miss Lottie Wilson, are not the ones who enjoy getting dirty. Here's a communication technique that might keep us out of the mud.

It is called, "I am your new best friend."

It works like this: "Gee, Ms. Payne, I would love to be able to give you those pills. I realize Doc Pushover gave you 300 Percocet a month. But you see, taking these pills year after year can cause damage to your innards, like your liver or your kidney. Gosh, if I wrote that prescription, I'd be hurting you, not helping you. And if something bad happened, I could never forgive myself. You see, Ms. Payne, I am your new best friend. What else, besides giving you these kinds of pills, could I do for you today?"

Okay.

I realize this won't work all the time.

These unlucky "Bowser chewed their Percocet" patients some-times are a lot cleverer than we are. Lots of times they have all the angles to outsmart us. So as long as we physicians and healers ply our trade, we'll find ourselves wallowing in the mud-wrestling pit.

All I'm saying is this: Let's wallow with a little more finesse.

CHALLENGING PATIENTS (CUSTOMERS)

WHY IT IS IMPORTANT KEEPING OUR COOL WITH CHALLENGING PEOPLE

Barbara is one of my most challenging patients. Although she has a very minor neurological problem, she is very focused on it. She demands that her doctors explore and explain each research update nugget she uncovers from Dr. Google.

Since her neurological issue involved some minor surgery, I referred Barbara to our neurosurgical center. A retired librarian (with a lot of time on her hands now), Barbara is as adept at cross-examination of doctors as she is at internet medical research. Suitcase full of cyber medical literature she arrived at the office of the neurosurgeon, Dr. Bill Sheridan. With her usual vigor and determination, the interrogation of Dr. Sheridan began. But the more she pressed him, the more relaxed Sheridan appeared. Barbara demanded explanations. Sheridan patiently explained. Barbara insisted on details. Sheridan calmly drew pictures.

On her follow-up visit with me a few days later, Barbara summed up her experience at the neurosurgical consultation.

"I was impressed with your Dr. Sheridan. I gave him a rough time," she admitted, "but he never lost his cool. He will be my surgeon. He must have a steady hand."

All this got me wondering.

When anxious and demanding people give us a difficult time, maybe they don't really mean to. Maybe it's all a test. Maybe they just want to know...

How steady is our hand?

LEARN TO "LAF" DEALING WITH ANGRY CUSTOMERS (PATIENTS)

I have an iron-clad rule about buying toys for my kids. Whatever I purchase must have these three magic words written on the box: "No Assembly Needed."

Several years ago, I broke this rule. I bought a snap-together Lego toy airplane model for my son Jeremy's birthday. My wife warned the neighbors to ignore the impending howls of despair that would soon emanate from our home.

Okay. So the inevitable happened. The company morons obviously screwed up their directions on Lego assembly. I went berserk. Neighbors two blocks away were closing their windows. I called the company, K'NEX Industries Inc. I spoke with customer service representative named Karen Mayberry. Years of frustration with the toy assembly industry exploded from the darkest netherworld of my psyche. It was not pretty.

Now Karen could have (appropriately) said three things:

1. Sir, if you continue to shout and use bad language, I will end this conversation.
2. Sir, if you threaten me or my company one more time, I will alert the police.
3. Sir, seventy-five thousand six-year-olds all across America have had no problem assembling this toy.

Instead Karen did three magical things:

26

1. She **L**istened. (I ranted, I vented, I felt better.)
2. She **A**pologized. "I am so sorry, Mr. Abramson," she said, "that you are having so much trouble with the assembly." (Notice that she apologized without necessarily admitting that it was the company's fault.)
3. She tried to **F**ix the problem. She asked if she could walk me through the directions (which she then proceeded to do).

Let me summarize Karen's three-step approach:

She **L**istened.
She **A**pologized.
She **F**ixed (at least tried to).
L.A.F.! Get it?

As we physicians and healers deal with our own difficult patients, perhaps we, too, need to learn to "LAF."

Addendum: I was so impressed with Karen's customer service techniques that I wrote a letter to the company, complimenting her. A few weeks later, the President of K'NEX Industries Inc., Mr. Norman Walker, wrote me back.

At the end of the letter, he wrote words of validation that I shall cherish to the end of my days. "Mr. Abramson," he confessed, "with my own daughter, I myself have had trouble building some of our models."

Now that's a real "LAF."

COMMUNICATION BREAKTHROUGH WITH A CHALLENGING PATIENT

Rhonda is a very challenging (read: difficult, exasperating) patient. She is twenty-five years old, a single mother with three young children. Her boyfriend is in jail. Her parents, with whom she lives, do not think highly of the young man who Rhonda considers the love of her life. It would be fair to say that they have made more than a few suggestions to Rhonda that perhaps she could have chosen more wisely as to who would father their grandchildren.

Rhonda is referred to me for intractable headaches. In a whimpering little-girl voice, Rhonda details endlessly her headaches. I make numerous helpful suggestions; Rhonda rejects them all.

I offer trials of pain-blocking-headache medication (Tricyclics, Neurontin, etc.).

Rhonda has had bad reactions to them all.

I suggest counseling. Rhonda says it makes things worse.

I advise stress management. Rhonda insists she has no stress.

Now in the old days, I would have cried uncle. I would have thrown up my hands, stormed out of the room, slammed the door, screamed at my medical assistant, and when I got home, slapped around my pet parakeet. But in our communication training, I recalled learning about some negotiating skills with a "challenging" patient. When you reach a roadblock with such a patient, so the teaching goes, confront them with the impasse. Let them know about your own frustration in trying to help. Put the ball back in their court.

I tried this communication advice.

"So, Rhonda," I began, "everything I suggest, you shoot down: the medication, the counseling, the stress reduction. I wish I could help, but I'm not sure how I can. I feel helpless. I feel frustrated. I feel trapped."

I figured these words summarized my reactions to this communication roadblock. Then alas, I think a breakthrough may have begun. For the first time in the visit, Rhonda actually looked at me. Her voice was different, more direct, more grown-up.

"Dr. Abramson," she answered, "now you know how I feel."

THE ONE THING YOU CAN NEVER LOSE

A while ago, I saw a movie (*Won't You Be My Neighbor?*) about the life of the children's TV icon, Mr. Fred Rogers.

"There is one thing you can never lose," said Mr. Rogers. "And that," he revealed, "is your childhood."

Shortly after I saw this movie, I had a serious disagreement with a fellow physician. I sent him an email; I left a message on his personal phone. I let him know I really needed to hear from him.

Day One: No response. I was irritated.

Day Two: No response. I was angry.

Day Three: Still no response. I was furious.

How could this guy ignore me? How could he disrespect me! Who the hell did he think he was! Not only was I enraged, I was feeling hurt and small.

This ate me up during those three days. I would awaken at 2:00 a.m. in a cold fury, ready to rip out his eyeballs, and eat them for a midnight snack! But on the fourth day, my colleague did call back. He apologized explaining he had had an out-of-town emergency. He regretted he had not left the update on his email or phone mail.

All this got me thinking. Why did I feel so furious, so hurt, so small, out of all proportion to the situation? And then I realized this fact: I had felt the same way lots of times when I was a child. And of course, like everybody else in the world, I did not have a perfect childhood. I had an older sibling who frankly terrified me. With just their tone of voice or a look, they could make me feel hurt and helpless and small. And I realized on those three days, in that interaction with my colleague, these same feelings came back to me. I was not just having a disagreement with another physician. I was being humiliated by my older sibling.

How painfully true for me were the words of Mr. Rogers. In those three days of confrontation with my colleague, I had never lost my childhood. In fact, I was wallowing in it. Or to put this in the words of William Faulkner, "The past is never dead. It is never even past."

I think Mr. Fred Rogers had it right. And maybe the lesson here was not to ignore the past or forget one's childhood, but instead to realize as deeply as we can how it can color every conversation, every interaction, every relationship in our lives.

"Everything that irritates us about others," said psychologist Carl Jung, "can lead us to an understanding of ourselves."

Or as my grandmother used to say, "Whenever you point your finger at someone, there are always three pointing back at you."

And maybe if we understand all that, just maybe, we won't be waking up at 2:00 a.m., feeling like ripping out the eyeballs of a fellow human being.

COMPLIMENTS
The Power of Praise

WHY MY PATIENT ASKED TO SEE A NEW DOCTOR

Betty, one of my memory-challenged patients, called our neurology clinic. She did not want to see me anymore. She now wanted to see a different neurologist. Then when she saw my colleague, this is what she told him:

"Dr. Abramson," Betty said, "may be a good doctor. But I do not like him. He asked me to remember three things, he told me to draw a clock, and he tested me on some math. During the entire time he tested my memory," she continued, "he never said I was doing okay on anything. I know I got some things right. But never once did he give me a word of praise."

And Betty was right.

I should have been able to say something nice.

I should have been able to utter an encouraging word.

Even those whose memories are impaired know the value of a compliment.

WHAT HAPPENS WHEN A MEDICAL ASSISTANT DOES THE RIGHT THING

On a holiday schedule, one of our pediatricians was working at a different medical station with a different medical assistant. A very anxious mom brought in her sick child. The medical assistant spent a lot of time comforting the frantic mom and calming the sick child. Now, in fact, this was nothing out of the ordinary for this particular medical assistant. Everyone who worked with her knew she was special. After the family had left, the visiting pediatrician invited the medical assistant into his office where he personally complimented her compassionate care of the mom and her child.

Guess what this medical assistant said upon hearing this compliment?

Nothing.

She uttered not one word.

She began to cry.

Why did this medical assistant cry?

I don't know.

But here is what I imagine:

In all those years of such extraordinary work, I wonder if any physician had ever taken a moment to give her such a genuine, heartfelt compliment. Oh sure, she often heard the perfunctory "Thanks, Jen, for rooming the patient" or "Thanks, Jen, for taking that temperature." But I wonder if any physician had ever given her such a personal, genuine, step-into-my-office compliment.

And maybe that is why, on this day, that compliment had so overwhelmed that medical assistant.

Here is a question: How often do we ask our medical assistants (or any of our team members) to step into our office for a special moment of praise?

"YOU MUST HAVE HAD A TOUGH DAY!"

I had a busy day. I sent out my last patient consult note after 9:00 p.m. to his treating hospital physician, Dr. Vijay Tiwari. The next morning, as we sat at adjacent computer terminals, Vijay leaned over and touched my shoulder.

"Gee whiz, Scott," he consoled me. "You sent me your consult note at 9:47 p.m. You must have had a tough day!"

What I instinctively answered was something like this: "Yeah, Vijay, it was a busy day. Had lots of consults, two stroke alerts, and then had to read EEGs from the weekend. I'm a slow typist, yada, yada, yada…"

So that was my response: explaining, justifying, even apologizing.

Afterward I thought about my instinctive answer. Here is what I realized:

Dr. Tiwari felt bad for my late hours and my heavy workload that night.

Dr. Tiwari cared about me.

Why was that so difficult for me to acknowledge?

Why did I have to explain or justify or even apologize?

Why couldn't I have simply answered…

"Thank you, Vijay. Thank you for caring."

I don't know. Maybe it's just me. But I have a hunch others may have difficulty accepting words of care from colleagues.

And I wonder.

Why is that?

"THE DOCTOR MADE ME FEEL SO HAPPY!"

Margaret had had a long time, unusual disabling neurodegenerative illness. Her husband was her devoted caregiver. Joe fed her, dressed her, and changed her diapers. They had seen numerous doctors, therapists, and specialists over the past years. Joe could hardly remember their names, much less their diagnostic impressions or medical advice. But there was one doctor among the many, one doctor that Joe spoke of with almost a supernatural reverence.

I was curious about this.

What made that doctor so wonderful?

I scanned the records.

Guess what that doctor wrote in his medical report?

Nothing. Nada. Zilch. Gornish. Bubkas.

The actual note of that doctor was just a scant few lines. It actually contained less information or insight than any other physician's note. So I asked Joe what was so special about that physician. Why was the visit with that particular doctor so powerfully etched in his mind?

"Well," replied the weary husband, a tough retired old longshoreman, now fighting back tears as he spoke, "that doctor made me feel so happy. 'Joe,' Doc told me, 'you're doing the best you can.'"

We all know the importance of giving our patients a compliment. But usually we compliment the observable, the tangible, the obvious.

"Nice cholesterol level, Mavis."

"Proud of you for that weight loss, Earl."

"Hey, Rocky, nice tattoo."

But how do we compliment the unobservable, the intangible, the unobvious?

How do we compliment a guy who is fighting a losing battle every day?

That's the challenge.

Maybe this doctor had the right idea.

"Joe," he says, "you're doing the best you can."

What better words could honor a caregiver?

"NOW WHAT HAPPENED?"

I was enjoying a Spanish omelet, hash browns with a side of blueberry pancakes at the Foster City IHOP. As I was about to leave the restaurant, a customer, standing at the register, asked the cashier to bring over the manager. He said he wanted to give some feedback on his waitress.

Approaching the customer, I heard the manager mutter under his breath, "Now what happened?"

However, it turned out the customer had had a really nice waitress. He told the manager how efficient and pleasant the waitress had been.

Then it dawned on me. The restaurant manager expected that when folks wanted to give feedback on food service, most of the time it was not positive. I suppose he had learned, statistically speaking, that folks were more likely to complain about service than compliment it. Not surprisingly when encountering feedback-giving customers, his natural reaction had become defensive: "Now what happened?"

And I understand this.

But it got me wondering.

How often do we make a special effort to give a compliment?

To our waitresses?

To our patients?

To our support staff?

To our colleagues?

To our spouses and life partners?

To our children?

When they see us approaching with feedback on our minds, how often are they silently muttering to themselves, wondering… "Now what happened?"

"GOOD ADVICE?"

Dr. Aneema Van Groenou observed that her thirteen-year-old teenage daughter seemed troubled.

"So tell me, Gisele," gently asked Aneema, "what's going on with you and your friend, Vanessa?"

"Oh, mom," replied Gisele, "You're just gonna give me 'good' advice."

"You mean," Aneema responded, "that it will be *my* advice."

"No, Mom," Gisele admitted. "It will be 'good' advice. But I just want you to agree with me. I just want you to tell me I'm right."

Thirteen-year-old Gisele had revealed to us a powerful truth: There is life-affirming satisfaction when someone agrees with you, when another human tells you that you are right. So what does this have to do with health care communication?

Consider this: Maybe we physicians, more than we know, miss the opportunity to bestow on our colleagues that same life-affirming satisfaction. Maybe we physicians miss lots of opportunities to simply tell our colleagues, "You are right."

For example, when specialists see consultations from primary care colleagues, they often are in total agreement with the referring doctors' evaluation. But how often in their consultation reports do specialists take the time to specifically write, "Dr. Lee, your patient has syndrome X. I agree one hundred percent with your diagnosis. You are right"?

How often in consultation reports do specialists take an extra five seconds to write the three words of magic "you are right"?

Imagine how this will affect Dr. Lee.

He will feel good, will he not?

When he gets home, Ms. Lee and the kids may feel that good karma.

And when Dr. Lee is feeling good, medical assistant Maria may feel those good vibes.

And when medical assistant Maria gets home, perhaps her family will feel them too.

Whatever we do in our personal or professional lives, it is a wonderful feeling when you hear those three magical words: "You are right."

Just ask Gisele.

COMRADERY

"IF I WOULD HAVE KNOWN..."

One of our doctors had been feeling overwhelmed, unappreciated, and frankly, just flat burned out. She decided to quit medicine. On her last day of work, many colleagues came over to say goodbye and to wish her well. We all told her how much we enjoyed working with her professionally. We told her how much we enjoyed knowing her personally.

"It's funny," the doctor half chuckled. "If I would have known that so many folks felt this way...I might not be leaving."

Here is a question: Why is it that our colleagues must be broken down, beaten up, and flat burned out before we can tell them how much we honor them as partners and as friends?

BEYOND THE CALL OF DUTY

A few months ago, one of my surgery colleagues told me he was feeling kind of ill. Nothing serious but just unwell. His surgical partner took call for him that night. Now that in itself was a beautiful gesture. But the way the surgeon found out his call would be covered was even more beautiful.

Here is how that happened.

The partner did not call Dr. X.

The partner knew macho-surgeon, Dr. X, would refuse the offer of help.

So instead Dr. X got a call from the hospital operator.

This was the message:

"Hello, Dr. X," the operator began. "Dr. Jones will be taking your call tonight. Please turn off your beeper. Good night, sir."

End of conversation.

Lots of times, for our patients, we physicians go beyond the call of duty. We do extraordinary things. Perhaps our colleagues deserve the same.

HOW TO MAKE A COLLEAGUE'S DAY GLORIOUS

Several years ago, I gave a talk on physician wellness at the South San Francisco Kaiser facility. The message I tried to spread was that, as Kaiser Permanente colleagues, we needed to support each other. After the talk, cardiologist Dr. Ed Fischer told me this story: "When I first joined Kaiser," he said, "like most other new docs, I was a little insecure and nervous. But a senior physician, a neurologist named Sid Rosenberg, gave me a helping hand. Whenever he saw me in the elevators or cafeteria or anywhere, Sid would tell me how much he appreciated my consults. He told me he had noted how hard I was working."

"And to this day," added Ed Fischer, "I remember those words of praise with profound gratitude."

I told Sid (who has now been retired several years) what Dr. Fischer had said.

Sid said I made his day.

In over thirty years at Kaiser Permanente, Dr. Rosenberg had seen a lot of neurology consults. I'm sure colleagues appreciated his expertise in diagnosing all sorts of things like cervical radiculopathies and cluster headaches and peripheral vestibulopathies. But I betcha Dr. Rosenberg never got as meaningful feedback from any consultation as he got on that day from Dr. Ed Fischer.

The power of praise: it can change lives.

EMPATHY

THE THREE MOST INTELLIGENT WORDS EVER SPOKEN BY A PHYSICIAN

During my neurology residency training program many years ago, I rotated through a hospital unit that was devoted to experimental multiple sclerosis therapy. The therapy involved the neurosurgical implantation of stimulating electrodes in the spinal cord. As the low man on the totem pole, first-year resident, my job was simply to interview these patients for their medical history, to do a physical examination and to document the progression of their multiple sclerosis. Once vigorous and productive, these folks had been cut down in their prime, often now strapped into their wheelchairs. They clung to any hope. They were desperate for any treatment.

Neurosurgeon Dr. Sergio Pacheco was my supervisor. The patients loved Dr. Pacheco. They trusted him. I did not think about it at the time, but looking back many years later, I think I understand now why Dr. Pacheco inspired such devotion. Inevitably, these patients would ask Dr. Pacheco the question that haunts so many of these devastated people:

"Why me?"

"Why me, Lord?"

"Why did this have to happen to me?"

Dr. Sergio Pacheco had the most intelligent response to this question I had ever heard. Sitting at their bedside, Dr. Pacheco would look into their eyes. He would shake his head sadly and then softly whisper these three words of wisdom:

The three most intelligent words I have ever heard a physician utter.

"I don't know," he would say.

"I don't know."

That was it.

Just three words.

His patients loved him.

His patients trusted him.

They had faith in his healing.

Many years later, like I had said, I think I understand why.

People don't want an answer. They know there is no answer.

All they want to know is…

Do we hear the question?

Are we there with them?

Dr. Sergio Pacheco heard the question.

He was there.

OPTION C

My friend Linda was diagnosed with a bad cancer. She went to see the cancer surgeon, Dr. Richard Godfrey, at Kaiser Fremont.

He laid out the options:

"Option A," he said, "we could do surgery first, then follow with chemo."

"Option B," he added, "we could shrink the tumor with chemo, then do surgery."

He was about to explain further when my friend (never one to sugarcoat anything) interrupted:

"Or," she shrugged hopelessly, "option C...we could do nothing."

Now at this point Dr. Godfrey could have done several things:

He could have explained more in detail about Option A or Option B.

He could have talked about the cancer in general.

He could have even discussed our excellent hospice program.

Instead, as my friend tells the story, Dr. Godfrey stopped typing on his computer.

He slowly turned his exam room stool to face her directly.

He looked in her eyes.

He took her hand.

He said softly, "Linda, let me help you."

Now I do not know the outcome of treatment.

It is still too early to tell.

"But in that moment," recalled my friend, "the healing began."

"YOU NEED TO LOSE 20 POUNDS!"

My wife's friend, Lilly, went for her Kaiser mammogram. She mentioned to the radiology doctor that she had some soreness in her breasts. The doctor replied immediately: "You need to lose 20 pounds."

Question: Guess what my wife's friend said?

Answer: Nothing.

Question: But guess how she felt when she heard these words?

Guess how she felt about the radiologist doctor who uttered those words?

Guess how she felt about the organization which hired this doctor who uttered those words?

Guess how many friends will hear about those words, the radiology doctor who uttered them, and the organization which hired him?

Answer: If I need to explain, you can skip the rest of this article.

And here's another question for all of us "always trying to be helpful" healers (and I plead as guilty as anyone): When we hear a problem, why is our natural instinct, our first response to solve it?

"Problem: Sore breasts."

"Solution: Lose 20 pounds."

That's how we do it, right?

(And of course we all know this doctor's two-second bit of advice will surely set Lilly hightailing it off to the neighborhood Curves Gym.)

But why must we always try to solve problems?

Why must we always try to *fix* stuff?

And what if this doctor, instead of spouting off the four-second lose-weight solution, what if he just gave the "knowing nod," acknowledging, but not fixing, the sore breast problem?

What if this doctor maybe even mumbled some sort of empathic word?

Sure, the soreness in Lilly's breasts would remain.

But maybe the hurt in her heart would not have begun.

"BODY ODOR"

I gave a presentation about the importance of expressing empathy in our communication with patients. I tried to stress the habit of trying to make just one empathic statement with every patient even if it's something like "Sorry, Ms. Garcia, about those rumblings in your tummy" or "That must be so tough, Mr. Jones, having those sniffles at night."

After the presentation, a physician approached me privately. He did not agree.

"If I'm not feeling empathy," he said, "it's not honest to speak the words. It's fake, it's phony, it's not me.

"It's not," he insisted, "*natural*."

Here was my response to this doctor. (Unfortunately, like so many of my brilliant retorts, I thought of this about thirty minutes after my colleague departed.)

But here is what *I wished* I would have said:

"Natural? You want natural? Let me give you natural. Body odor is natural! But most of us wear fresh clothes. We take showers. We put on deodorant."

All I'm saying is...

In conversation with our patients, let's put on a little deodorant. What's "unnatural" about dabbing a little Old Spice on that?

CONNECTING WITH OUR PATIENTS: CONTINUING PHYSICIAN EDUCATION

Debbie Moore, one of our nurse practitioners, asked me to come over to the oncology clinic to evaluate one of her new cancer patients, a patient who she suspected might be having some neurological complications of that cancer. Debbie remained with me in the exam room while I examined Esther, her very worried patient.

I took an extensive neurological history. I did a detailed neurological exam. I explained to Esther the comprehensive differential diagnosis. I carefully outlined the ensuing diagnostic tests and possible treatments. I felt good afterward. I had just completed another neurological consultation. I was certain that even though Esther still remained quite worried, she had to be impressed by my expertise. And as an added bonus, I was delighted that Nurse Practitioner Debbie Moore had the opportunity to observe such a conscientious neurologist plying his trade. I was sure it would further her continuing medical education.

Now, as Debbie and I were about to leave the exam room, something magical happened. Debbie took Esther's hand and grasped it between both of hers.

"Try not to worry, Esther." Debbie smiled warmly. "We'll take care of you."

For the first time since the consultation began, Esther looked visibly calmed. She hugged Debbie. She thanked her. Then we all said goodbye.

It's funny.

I did all the right doctor-specialist stuff: the history, the examination, the differential diagnosis, the work-up, the discussion, the treatment options…all were performed flawlessly.

I was a technical wiz, I got all the technical, the tangible stuff…

But what I missed was the untechnical, the intangible…

What I missed was making a genuine connection with our patient.

Touching, smiling, words of caring, that's what making connections with patients is about.

I thank you, Nurse Practitioner Debbie Moore, for another lesson in my own continuing medical education.

"BUT JUST ONCE..."

Susan's husband was diagnosed with cancer. In addition to continuing to work her full-time job, now Susan had the new burden of caring for Bob. Susan spent a lot of time at the hospital. She spent a lot of time talking with doctors and specialists and nurses.

Bob died two years later.

I asked Susan what it was like for her during all those conversations with the medical world. I knew Bob had been given excellent medical care at our hospital, but I wondered how we had scored in our communication of that care. I wondered how we'd scored on the empathy meter.

"Oh," replied Susan, "the doctors and the nurses were wonderful to Bob. They were kind. They were caring. They were compassionate."

"But just once in all that time," Susan added, "I wish they would have asked about *me*."

HOW A TELEPHONE OPERATOR HELPED ME OVERCOME ILLNESS

Over thirty years ago, I had the only serious illness of my life. I was off work for six weeks. It was an unusual condition, and because it was so atypical, I was not only seen in consultation by specialists at my own hospital, but I was also sent to the local university hospital for their expert opinion. I also personally telephoned specialists in this field all over the country. It turned out there was really nothing anyone could do. I was told it would heal with time. (It did.)

To be honest, almost as bad as the illness itself was the frustration of being helpless and unable to work, and the guilt about letting down patients and colleagues. I admit, during these six weeks, I was probably not the most pleasant guy in the solar system. Even my beloved wife (who was forced to be my designated driver in those weeks) seemed to get a bit testy as I offered constructive criticism and helpful suggestions to improve her driving skills.

Periodically I would call my hospital to try to keep in touch with my practice. Whenever Alice Merrick, one of our telephone operators, took my call, she always said something that helped me in those difficult days.

"Doctor Abramson," she would say, "I am so sorry you are sick."

In those six weeks I spoke to many expert doctors and professors. But only a telephone operator took the time to utter words of empathy.

WHY I FAILED TO CURE MY WIFE'S HEADACHE

I work as a neurologist. This came in handy because on a Saturday morning a while ago, my wife awoke with a headache. Now deep down I knew this was nothing serious. But I also knew you can't be objective when treating family members. My old neurology chief once warned me, "Never treat your secretary or your wife."

So I knew what had to be done. I whirled into action. I ran from our bedroom to the kitchen phone. I dialed our local Kaiser hospital. I would prime the local ER we'd be coming in. I would get a CT-STAT. I would get a consultation from my neurological on-call colleague. I would take care of business. I would do my doctor shtick. I would "find it." I would "fix it."

I mean because that is what I do! Pamela would be so proud. (Okay...And for once she would finally have to admit I could do something useful around the house.)

So I wait on the kitchen phone through five minutes of phone mail hell. I was unable to speak to anyone of the human persuasion. I gave up. I trudged back to the bedroom. Lo and behold, the headache had now gone away. But Pamela didn't even look at me. She was furious. "Where did you run off to? All I wanted was a little attention."

True enough. I spent five minutes waiting on a telephone line trying to do what I always do: "Find it, fix it."

But suppose I had spent the same five minutes at Pamela's bedside just giving..."a little attention"?

Heck, instead of Doctor Zero, I would have been Husband Hero!

But sure enough.

This is not about winning brownie points with our spouse.

This is about understanding our patients. They don't always need "find it...fix it."

Sometimes, like Pamela, all they need is..."a little attention."

COMPASSION: LESSON FROM A POST OFFICE CLERK

The U.S. Post Office screwed up my mail. The postal clerk told me there was nothing that could be done. She said she could not help me. And then she laid out all the reasons why. I'm sure she was probably right. But I felt angry, not just because my mail delivery was screwed up, but because her manner was so mechanical, so robotic. I counted to ten; I calmed my anger. And then in the most pleasant tone of voice I could muster, I gave her this customer feedback:

"Ma'am, I realize you are likely correct in what you told me. I realize you are unable to help me. But your demeanor lacked any empathy for my predicament. Your tone of voice lacked any trace of compassion. Have a nice day." Then I turned and walked away.

But later on, I thought this: How often have I myself, seen patients that I have been unable to help? And in those situations, how often did my demeanor lack empathy for them? How often did my tone of voice lack any trace of compassion?

THE MYTH OF COMPASSION FATIGUE

My dear physician colleagues:

Look over the schedule of the patients you have already seen today. As you recall each patient, ask yourself this question: in that encounter, did I truly feel toward my patient genuine compassion?

I will be brutally honest with you (and myself). For me, on many days, that figure is maybe, at best, about 5 percent.

It's tough. We are running thirty minutes late. Three irritated, waiting-room patients yearn for our presence. Our inbox has thirteen secure messages, twelve refills, seven staff messages, three handicapped parking requests, two jury excuse letters, and four demands for off work slips. And of course, we get monitored and we get graded on how efficiently we handle all this. The daily hustle can be overwhelming. And then we must leave the clinic in time to pick up our kids in day care before the late fee kicks in. We worry whether we'll be home for dinner or whether the family will eat without us…*again*. So when our patients come to us with run-of-the-mill, mundane, low-back pain, tension headaches, or nighttime coughs, in those encounters do we feel genuine…*compassion*? As for myself, most of the time, I confess: I do not.

We often explain and excuse this by pleading, "Compassion fatigue."

I take this to mean that we give so much compassion, day in and day out, that we are tapped out. We no longer have any more compassion to give. Our compassion tank is drained.

I disagree.

"Compassion fatigue" is a myth.

We don't give *too much* compassion.

We are so overwhelmed with the daily doctor hustle that we don't have the time or the inclination to give much compassion in the first place.

It's not "compassion fatigue."

It's "Lucy in the Chocolate Factory" fatigue!

Like Lucy in the Chocolate Factory our minds are focused on not much else, but the next batch of electronic medical data products rolling down the health care assembly line.

So how do we bring genuine caring to our patients? How can we express compassion even on those "Lucy in the Chocolate Factory" days? How can we raise our compassion meter from 5 percent to 50 percent or to 95 percent even as we struggle in the Kaiser Inbox Fatigue syndrome?

I know the answer.

The answer is simple.

Yet it is difficult.

It takes one crucial flip of the mind switch. I bet most of you already know what I'm talking about. I bet most of you already know the answer. I knew it too. But recently a young woman rekindled my appreciation of this profound truth. Christina Lewis works in our Pleasanton Kaiser Member Assistance program. (Read "complaint department.") I asked her how she dealt with all the angry, frustrated patients who often would lash out at her personally for their long waits in the physician waiting room, for the nightmare search for a parking spots, for the endless wait for the doctor office callback, etc.

Christina responded to my question with a simple but potentially life-changing answer. I don't think there is any more important wisdom in the physician-patient communication realm than the words I heard her speak next.

"*I put myself,*" said Christina, "*in their shoes.*"

"I try to imagine myself," continued Christina, "waiting an hour for the doctor in the waiting room, knowing I'm late to pick up my daughter in day care. I think of myself spending twenty-five frazzled minutes finding parking. I think of myself waiting anxiously at home for the doctor's phone call, worried sick about my child's health. *I put myself in their shoes.*

"Yes, sometimes our patients can be tough," continued Christina, "but I love my job."

So if, like Christina, we can put ourselves in our patient's shoes, then we, too, may feel more compassion for those folks with a cough that robs sleep. If we try to walk in our patient's shoes, perhaps we, too, may feel more sympathy for those whose backache keeps them from playing catch with their son or those who lie awake at night wondering if the tension headache is a bursting brain tumor.

If we try to walk in our patient's shoes, perhaps then we, too, will be able to feel more compassion. Perhaps we, too, may have more love for our job.

And perhaps we, too, may find in our daily work lives more joy and meaning.

And while I will sing amen to this choir, I know I am a sinner. I know I will struggle even today trying to walk in the shoes of my afternoon's fifth worried, well-dizzy patient.

But if you, my physician brothers and sisters, looked back on your schedule today and found yourself walking in your patient's shoes, if you, like Christina Lewis, do this regularly and are finding for your patients' genuine compassion, then God bless you.

I wish I could.

But I'll still try.

Every day.

Every patient.

FAITH

"NOW I KNOW I HAVE A FATHER"

I worked for many years at the Kaiser hospital in the Sleepy Hollow neighborhood of Hayward, California. It was a pretty rough neighborhood. There were the usual issues with drugs and alcohol, teen pregnancies, vagrancy, whatnot. We had our local neighborhood gang called, "The Sleepy Hollow Boys." Suffice it to say, just to play it safe, I never stopped and lingered at the nearby 7-Eleven after the sun went down.

One of these neighborhood kids was my patient, eighteen-year-old Darren. Like many kids from the neighborhood, he had grown up in a single-parent home. While Darren had in the past done his share of gangbanging, now he had turned his life around. He was bussing tables at the Olive Garden restaurant. He was going to night school to become a plumber. He looked forward to some-day raising a family of his own. Unlike his own male biological sperm donor, Darren looked forward to someday being a real father to his own son.

I asked what had changed his life.

Darren told me about a neighborhood preacher who had reached out to him. The preacher had spoken about a God in heaven who loved him.

"I now know for the first time," said Darren, "that I have a Father. I have a Father who cares about me. I have a Father who cares whether I do good or whether I do bad. I want to do good."

If troubled young men, like Darren, believe they have a Father in heaven, a Father who cares whether they do good or whether they do bad, then I believe America will be a better place.

Perhaps then no one will ever be afraid to stop and linger at the local 7-Eleven.

Anytime.

Anywhere.

Even in the Sleepy Hollow neighborhood of Hayward, California.

THE FIRST SURGEON

A friend of mine went into the hospital for a surgical operation. Afterward Ruth told me about the talk she had with her doctors. Meeting with her surgeon and her anesthesiologist prior to surgery, this retired lifelong Sunday school teacher could not resist the temptation to give them both a Bible lesson.

"Let me ask you doctors," she inquired, "who do you think performed the first surgery?"

As the doctors pondered this, looking a bit puzzled, Ruth answered simply: "God."

(Though when Ruth said the word, it came out in about three syllables.)

"God," she continued, "was the first surgeon. He took Adam's rib and made Eve."

"After this," added Ruth, "every surgery has been performed by humans. And as you perform my surgery this day, may God guide your hand."

Now I realize many of us in the medical profession are of the secular persuasion. A lot of this "God" and "Jesus" and "Hallelujah" stuff we don't relate to.

I get that.

On the other hand, perhaps we need to honor those people of faith, like my friend Ruth: people who have faith that God is guiding our hands.

WHAT HAPPENED AT WENDY'S

I ate dinner at Wendy's.

A couple had just gotten their meal.

The guy wore a work shirt with the name "Bob" printed above the left breast pocket.

The woman was missing a tooth or two. They sat beside each other. They held hands.

They bowed their heads.

They said grace.

They thanked God for His beneficence.

It's funny.

I have eaten in many upscale restaurants. These restaurants are patronized by men whose shirt pockets did not reveal their first names and by women whose mouths had a full complement of teeth. I never saw anyone in those places ever bow their heads in grateful prayer.

I wonder why.

FEEDBACK
(Including That Which I Give Myself)

"NEXT TIME YOU CALL ME..."

They say when someone gives you criticism...it is a "gift."

Recently the husband of one of my patients gave me just such a well-deserved gift.

As a neurologist dealing with all sorts of folks who faint or pass out for whatever reason, it is most crucial to get the eyewitness history. Since the patients often come to see me alone, I find myself then telephoning the spouse or eyewitness to get the exact details of the event, most importantly to explore whether this might be an epileptic seizure.

Recently I saw a young woman in such a situation. As she sat in my exam room, I contacted her husband by telephone to get the lowdown on what exactly happened. The husband, obviously very concerned, answered all my questions. As with most of these cases, fortunately it turned out there was nothing serious. It was not epilepsy. It was just a simple faint.

At the end of the conversation, however, just as we were about to hang up, the husband bestowed upon me his "gift."

"Just one thing, Doc," he added. "Next time you call me...first tell me my wife is okay."

Oh my gosh.

I have been doing this same darn thing all my career. I never stopped to think about those first moments of panic when a loved one receives...

"The Doctor's Phone Call."

Now I do things differently. Now in the first words I speak, I reassure family that their loved ones are safe in my office and in no danger.

Just goes to show.

It's never too late to accept a gift.

JULIA'S GIFT

Julia is a fun-loving single gal and avid Oakland A's fan. Over the two years she has been my patient, she has been devastated by the ravages of multiple sclerosis. She is now confined to a wheelchair. But Julia is full of spunk and determination. Though she struggles mightily, she still manages to live independently. She combs the internet to find any device that might aid her in this struggle. I then dutifully pursue these requests through our DME (durable medical equipment) department.

Many times I have had long back-and-forth conversations with DME personnel to clarify the details of these requests. I must confess: some of the intricate, detailed specifics of these equipment orders were getting to be a little annoying. And truth be told, all this was taking up a lot of my precious doctor time. I was beginning to feel less like a specialist physician and more like a health care butler.

I suspected one of my email conversations with Julia, she may have picked up on this attitude. In her next email equipment request, she concluded with these exact words: "Dr. Abramson, I trust that you will continue to be my advocate."

And Julia was right.

I should be her advocate.

That is my job.

But sometimes, like many of us, I get overwhelmed by the excruciating details of a routine doctor's busywork.

I forget.

I forget my job.

I forget that my real job, above all else, is to be my patient's advocate.

Thank you, Julia, for this reminder.

Thank you for this gift

I am humbled to receive it.

BEING RIGHT

I saw a patient in neurology clinic whose symptoms and whose examination clearly indicated to me he must have a growth or a tumor on his spine. I wrote that presumed diagnosis in my consultative note. I sent that note back to his referral doctors. I was proud of myself. It was a peculiar case, and I had made the correct assessment. I ordered an MRI scan of the spine to confirm my brilliant diagnosis. Two days later, much to my surprise, it came back normal. No tumor. No blood clots. No abscess. No nothing. The spine was completely normal!

My first reaction? A part of me felt disappointed. A part of me felt angry. By gosh, I had made a diagnosis of spinal tumor, the guy should have had one! Who the heck did he think he was? The nerve of him!

Then the "omigosh" moment hit me.

Instead of being relieved my patient had no spine tumor, I felt disappointed because I was flat-out wrong.

Sometimes I forget.

This is not about the physician in me who seeks scientific rightness.

It is about the humanity in me which should be seeking my patients' healing.

FUNERALS...
DEATH...
BEREAVEMENT

THE MOST IMPORTANT WORDS ONE CAN SAY TO THE BEREAVED

Diana has a benign, very stable neurological condition for which she sees me on routine yearly visits. On one such visit, her husband asked to speak with me privately before I saw Diana.

"My wife is devastated beyond recognition," he told me. "Two months ago, while riding his bike, our eighteen-year-old son was killed by a drunk driver."

I saw Diana that morning. Ghostlike, she mumbled her way through the appointment. Then she left.

One year later I saw Diana again. On the surface, she seemed back to her usual engaging and animated self. She explained she was counseling other parents whose children had been tragically killed. I was intrigued by this.

"Diana," I said, "you have been on both sides. You, yourself, have lost a child, and now you console others with a similar loss. What can you possibly say in such a situation? What words could comfort a mother or a father who has suffered such a nightmare? What is the secret?"

Not just as a physician, but in my personal life. I often feel uncomfortable visiting the homes of the bereaved. I never know quite what to say. So I eagerly awaited Diana's words of advice.

And I have cherished Diana's words of wisdom since that moment.

"As to what I say when I comfort others," explained Diana, "I have only one secret. It is simply this: You don't have to say anything. Ninety-nine percent of it...is just being there."

"EVEN THE DOCTOR CAME!"

Joanne died last week. She was only fifty-two years old. In those last years, stricken by a relentlessly progressive neurological disease, she was wheelchair-bound, hardly able to speak or eat or even control her bodily functions. In truth, a part of me began to view her clinic appointments...well (I am not proud to say this)...with a kind of helpless annoyance.

One of my mentors and role models, Dr. Gerald Peters, went to almost all of his patients' funerals.

He did it for two reasons: "First," said Gerry, "my attendance as a physician, I believe, honors my patients. At the funeral service I've heard the whisper of family and friends: 'Look, even the doctor came!'"

"And second," Gerry smiled, "I do this for myself. I need to be reminded that my patients have had a life outside of their medical appearances at my office."

So I went to Joanne's funeral. Three hundred folks were packed in the chapel. There was not an empty pew. The pastor asked all those who had ever had a meal cooked by Joanne at Bible study to stand up. One hundred or so then stood. Then the pastor asked all those to stand whose home had been visited by Joanne when a family member was ill. Another hundred or so stood up.

Finally the pastor asked all those to stand who had ever had their baby feet kissed by Joanne. About twenty young folks, mostly nieces and nephews, children and teens and young adults, arose. Now just about everyone in the church, three hundred strong, stood in silent testimony.

Maybe Gerry Peters was right. Perhaps attending our patients' funerals is as important for the soul of the healer as it is for the tribute to the departed.

Perhaps I needed reminding that the parched lips of this ill-stricken woman once upon a time so joyously kissed the toes of countless giggling babies.

WHEN DEATH IS INEVITABLE: HOW PHYSICIANS CAN STILL BRING HEALING

My cousin Ken died. At age sixty-four, he had passed after a courageous battle with pancreatic cancer. During his last days in the hospital, Ken was surrounded at the bedside by many loved ones. On the day he died, one particular doctor came by. He had performed a minor procedure earlier in the week. Now there was clearly nothing more that could be done by this doctor (or any doctor for that matter).

"I just wanted to come by," said the doctor. "I wanted to tell you that even though I met Ken only during this last week, it was a privilege to know you folks. To have such loving family and friends, Ken truly must have been someone special."

Maybe there's a message here for us physicians and healers:

In those last days, when death is inevitable, when things are hopeless, there is, after all, perhaps one thing that can be done.

Perhaps in that moment, we can take the time to honor the devotion of loved ones.

THE PSEUDO-OBITUARIES

Many folks regularly read the local obituary column. My mother did. Every morning she'd open the local paper, turn to the obituary page, and first thing, she would check to make sure her name wasn't in there.

"Well," she would smile, "the day is starting out swell!"

Sometimes I bet we've heard folks read the obit columns and say things like "Gosh, old man Johnson died yesterday. Didn't even know he was sick. Would have liked to say goodbye to the old guy." Or...

"Gee whiz, Ms. Jones just passed. She was the best doggone history teacher I ever had. Wish I could have told her how much she meant to me."

Here's an idea.

How about a "Pseudo-Obituary" news page?

How about a daily newspaper column that, instead of reporting the dead, reports the "Almost Dead"?

Folks might think, "Hey, lookee here. Ms. Jones, my old history teacher, is in the hospital. I'll drop by to pay my respects. Tell her I'm sorry about throwing those spitballs in study hall."

Or...

"Gosh. Says here in paper old man Johnson is real sick. Think I'll drop by to say goodbye. Besides it's been twenty-three years, and I never returned that darn weed whacker."

I don't know.

It just seems to me if we really want to say a final goodbye to someone, doesn't it make sense to do it at the bedside instead of the gravesite?

I NEVER WROTE THE LETTER

Even in our private lives, at cocktail parties, Little League games, yoga classes, when folks find out we are physicians, somehow they often feel compelled to tell us their very own health care sagas. Some time ago while I was waiting in a Starbucks' line, a young woman noted my hospital name badge. She then told me her story:

"My dad had cancer," she said. "He spent the last fifteen months of his life…dying…at your hospital. My dad received excellent medical care. The doctors and nurses were wonderfully compassionate. My dad suffered, but everyone was so nice and caring.

"Dad died about one month ago. I was planning to write a letter expressing my thanks for all the doctors and nurses had done. But after he died, I heard not one word from your hospital. Not one phone call. Not one condolence card. Doctors and nurses showed such great concern while he was dying; yet after his death, it was as if he never existed. I felt hurt. I felt abandoned. I never wrote the letter."

Consider this.

When we make a commitment to give our patients full and meaningful care, perhaps this does not end at their death.

HEROES

WHAT AIRLINE PILOTS AND PHYSICIANS DON'T APPRECIATE

As soon as we land from an airplane flight, why do most of us call our loved ones back home to tell them we arrived safely? Most folks, I suspect, are like me, grateful to have landed without anything bad happening. I am not afraid of flying, but I do have a healthy respect for being thirty thousand feet in the air with my life depending on the expertise of the two human beings who pilot the plane. And I would bet that most folks, like me, perhaps once or twice during that flight, have a passing thought about what would happen if the efficiency of those two humans or the machine they pilot were to somehow fail.

That is why after we have landed and as I exit the plane, I always personally thank the pilot. At that moment I feel toward him genuine gratitude. At that moment, he is my hero.

But to the pilot, I suspect, my authentic expression of gratitude is "nothing special." Hundreds of passengers each day probably give him the same thank-you. I doubt he appreciates how grateful to him folks like me are feeling for landing safely. I doubt he feels like a hero.

As physicians and healers hundreds of our own passengers "land safely" each week. They may "land safely" from bouts of acid indigestion or runny noses or sprained ankles. It's all in a routine, ordinary, mundane workday for us.

But maybe not for our patients.

How many of us take real satisfaction from their genuine thank-yous?

How many of us feel good about doing the "nothing special"? It's too bad airline pilots don't appreciate they are heroes. Too bad for us physicians and healers too.

WHERE HAVE ALL THE HEROES GONE?

One Sunday evening, I noted on my cheek a small dark mole. I had an instantaneous and horrific premonition: it was a malignant melanoma. Not mentioning a word of this discovery to my wife, I silently left the house that night. I walked for hours along the Alameda shoreline.

The next morning, I made the obligatory dermatology appointment, an appointment that I knew would confirm the dreaded diagnosis. Dr. Gary Dick looked at the brown mole on my cheek. Reaching from his instrument tray, he took a small lancet to the nodule.

"That's it, Scott," he said. "Just a little blood blister. Take care, buddy."

He patted my shoulder and went on to his next patient. It was a busy morning for him.

That was it?...

A "blood blister"?

"Take care, buddy."?

Dr. Gary Dick had just given me back my life! I wept silent tears of rebirth. I was ready to fall to my knees and kiss the hem of his Kaiser Permanente issue lab coat.

Now this happened over thirty years ago. But I recall it as if it were yesterday. I remember the sudden terror of self-diagnosis as I looked in the mirror that Sunday night. I remembered the all-night walk up and down the Alameda shoreline, pondering my terminal diagnosis. I remembered the kiss I gave my two-year-old son as I left to meet my fate that Monday morning. And looking back on this, here's what I'm wondering:

On that dermatology appointment, in those few moments that so changed my life, did Dr. Gary Dick have the slightest clue of what he did for me?

Did he get much satisfaction from that visit?

Did he experience personal rapture about his job?

Did he feel like a hero?

Frankly I doubt he did. Bust a blood blister on a neurotic colleague and on to the next patient.

No, I suspect Dr. Dick didn't feel particularly glorious about that Monday-morning-pimple pop.

But he should have.

He should have felt like a hero.

Because he was one.

To me.

And though, like Dr. Gary Dick, we may think nothing of it, we are the real-life heroes to so many of our patients. We are heroes for all the mundane, ordinary, nitpicking, scut puppy, blister-popping stuff we do.

So let's honor ourselves as heroes.

I wish Dr. Dick had.

He deserved it.

And so do we.

"AH, YOU ARE MY 7:30 A.M. PATIENT"

One of my colleagues was a particular health-conscious guy. He jogged about seventy miles a day and eats truckloads of broccoli sprouts. One day at age fifty-eight, while jogging, he blew out his left knee. Now of course he understood that in the scope of medical problems, this was not such a big deal. But the injury shattered his self-image of vitality. He was devastated. He realized he was no longer invincible. He felt vulnerable.

He underwent surgery. Everything went fine. He counted the days till his physical therapy. He was determined to regain his vitality. He would do whatever it took. He would work double hard. He arrived at the physical therapy clinic eagerly awaiting his first appointment. The therapist looked at the registration slip and said, "Ah, you are my 7:30 a.m. patient."

The doctor shook his head.

"No," he answered. "I am not your 7:30 a.m. patient. I am the man to whom you will give his life back!"

Here's a question to all of us physicians and healers: when we look at our own schedules, do we see our patients as the 7:30 a.m. patient?

Or do we see them as men and women to whom we will give some part of their life back?

AN ANESTHESIOLOGIST'S GIFT OF THE "NOTHING SPECIAL"

Twenty-nine years ago on a Sunday night, my eleven-month-old son began vomiting and screaming with spasms of tummy pain. It turned out Jeremy had an intussusception of the bowel (which, as we learned that night, means the bowel was blocked as it twisted on itself). As we held Jeremy in our arms that night in the emergency room, my wife and I were terrified. The on-call surgeon lived a good distance away. He would not be in for at least an hour.

But on call, and still in the hospital, was a very experienced anesthesiologist, Dr. Jo Von Pohl. He sat with us. He said something that to this day I have not forgotten. And to this day I cannot remember any words that ever meant more to me.

"Scott," he smiled, "I will take good care of your son."

It is twenty-nine years later.

Why do I write this now?

For one thing, even to this day, even now as I write, I think of that night. I think of Dr. Von Pohl's words of healing reassurance. I think of those words with the most profound gratitude.

But I also think about this:

Dr. Jo Von Pohl over the years had put thousands of babies and children and grown folks to sleep and woken them up. That night, to him, may have been a routine night's work. It may have been, to him, "nothing special."

And I wonder if we physicians, too, feel sometimes our everyday work is "routine." I wonder if we feel sometimes, what we say and what we do is "nothing special."

And perhaps some days, for us, it may seem like that.

But maybe not for our patients.

For them our routine "nothing special" work may forever live in their grateful memories.

To that, my family bears witness.

INSPIRATION

THE BEAUTY OF A CROOKED SMILE

Maria works as an aide in a nursing home. She spends many hours changing the diapers of lots of old and sick folks. I saw her in the neurology clinic because the right side of her face had become paralyzed, a condition we call Bell's palsy. When I saw her, it was one month after the paralysis began, and the right side of her face was still partly paralyzed. Though the paralysis usually gets better with time, Maria was worried it might not. But she was worried for a different reason than most.

"Doctor Abramson," she confided, "I'm afraid I won't get my smile back. And sometimes, Doctor, for my patients, all I have to give...is a smile."

Those were her words.

Let me repeat them:

"Sometimes for my patients, Doctor, all I have to give...is a smile."

(And we are talking about giving a smile to sick, old folks who probably can't even remember her name.)

If I were in Maria's place and my face was paralyzed and disfigured, I can guarantee you, those would not be my words.

Yet I cannot help but have this thought:

When I meet folks like Maria, I am humbled by their beauty.

I am humbled by their beauty no matter how crooked the smile.

"ONE THING I WILL NEVER DO!"

At age sixty Laura now has suffered over thirty years of devastating attacks of multiple sclerosis. She hardly has any feeling in her legs, legs so weakened that in anyone else, they would render them wheel-chair-bound. But amazingly, with foot braces and with crutches, Laura keeps walking.

Here is her secret:

"Whenever a paralyzing attack of MS comes," said Laura, "there is absolutely one thing I will not do: I will not get into the bed!"

"Believe me," she continued, "it would be the easiest thing in the world to do. I have a very supportive husband. I have wonderful children. They would care for me. They would wait on me hand and foot. But no matter how bad the attack, I will not get into that bed. I sleep on the floor. I eat on the floor. I crawl on the floor. I will not get into that bed."

It's funny.

We physicians often say our rewards come from making a difference in our patients' lives. Sometimes it works the other way too. Sometimes our patients, by their courage, by their tenacity, and by their grace, can inspire a difference in ours.

"NOT AT THIS TIME"

At age forty-two, Keith had suffered a severe stroke. He was completely paralyzed on his left side. As I examined him (with his sister at his hospital bedside), he answered my medical questioning in a way I had never quite heard before. I asked him if he could move his left arm.

He responded, "Not at this time."

I asked him if he could move his leg. He repeated, "Not at this time."

I asked if he could move his toes. Again, the same response: "Not at this time."

In all my years of neurology practice no one has ever responded to me in quite this way. Either they say "no" or they say "yes" and then proceed to show me how they move it.

I wondered about that peculiar response. Later on I spoke to the sister. She cleared up the mystery.

"My brother," she told me, "is a natural-born fighter. In his twenties he was near-death with what his doctors told him was incurable cancer. Keith beat the cancer. Since then, in addition to his usual job, he gives motivational speeches, trying to give others inspiration and hope. When you asked him if he could move his left arm and his left leg, he knew he could not. He knew he was totally paralyzed. So when Keith answered, 'not at this time,' what he was telling you, Doctor, is that he will never accept that verdict. What he was saying is that he will never, never, ever give up!"

Addendum: after I wrote this piece folks asked me what happened to Keith?

Let me give you two answers. You can choose which to accept:

1. I don't know. After hospital discharge he went to a rehab hospital and from there, discharged to a different Kaiser facility. I am sorry to say I did not get a follow-up.
2. With every fiber of my being, I do believe, as did Keith, that he would beat this thing.

"I TAKE CARE OF SICK PEOPLE"

A young man came into our clinic perched atop a wheelchair seat. The reason he was "perched" was because the young man had no legs. After a childhood accident, his legs had been amputated just below the hips. We took care of the minor incidental neurological issue for which he was referred, and then we talked a little Oakland Raider football. But Raul seemed restless and eager to leave my office.

"Got to go, Doc," he said. "I work in a board and care facility. I take care of sick people."

WHAT OTHER PARENTS GET TO DO THIS?

Jason is now thirty-five years old. He was born with a damaged brain. He says only a few words. He can walk a little with a walker but mostly stays in a wheelchair. His parents change his diapers. Occasionally, if upset, Jason will smear feces, but overall, his parents say he is a happy guy. His dad brought Jason into my neurology clinic on this get-acquainted visit. Dad said Jason loves his old faded Green Bay Packer cap, and he loves to go to Disneyland.

His parents, now in their late sixties, have devoted their life to his daily care.

I mentioned to dad how tough this must have been for them.

"Oh no." Dad smiled. "Gee whiz, we are so grateful. What other parents, for thirty-five years running, get to take their kid to Disneyland!"

It's tough being a physician these days. Long hours in the hospital and even more hours of take-home work on our hospital laptops. We often feel worn-out and discouraged. But what if we, amidst our own tough doctor days, were grateful for our own Disneylands, Disneylands that are there for us every single day?

JARGON: WORDS ARE IMPORTANT

"FRISCO"

Two guys were sleeping in a San Francisco Park. (This is a true story. It must be. I read it in the SF Chronicle newspaper.) A policeman approached.

"Where you fellas from?" the cop inquired.

The fellas answered, "Frisco."

The cop arrested them. Later at the station house, it was found they were both escaped convicts from Colorado.

Question: How did the cop know the fellas were lying?

Answer: Nobody from San Francisco ever calls it, "Frisco."

(This would be like a New Yorker saying they are from "The Big Apple" or a native of Chicago saying they are from "The Windy City.")

Lesson: Words have consequences.

Whatever our careers, whether we are health care clinicians…or escaped convicts from Colorado, words have consequences.

JARGON: WORDS THAT DON'T WORK

THE DANGER OF "DOCTORSPEAK"

A while ago I happened to witness a family hospital conference about their dad's new diagnosis of cancer. There were ten family members present, all very devoted and concerned, though not particularly medically sophisticated. With much compassion and patience the hospital physician reported that the X-rays showed what was almost certainly a newly discovered cancer.

The doctor pointed out the multiple brain lesions on the MRI. She informed the family about other lesions showing up in the bone and still more lesions in the liver. The primary lesion, she suspected, was most likely in the lung. She then explained how lesions could spread from the primary to different parts of the body. The family listened respectfully, but they seemed more than a bit puzzled by it all. Suddenly one brave family member blurted out, "What's a lesion?"

For a moment the doctor looked crestfallen. It occurred to her that in the last five minutes, nothing she said had been understood. Then she made a brilliant recovery.

"A lesion," she promptly declared, "is a cancer spot."

She then went through the same spiel again, but this time, instead of the word "lesion" she substituted the term, "cancer spot." This time, as she spoke, the family nodded with understanding. When the doctor had finished her explanation, the family, though clearly saddened by the bad news, asked about the possibility of treatment.

"Good question," replied the doctor, "but first we need to get *tissue.*"

"LOW PRIORITY"

I was working on a Physician Wellness Committee project. I needed administrative support. Things were not moving too swiftly. I emailed administration for a status report.

Here was the message I got back:

"Sorry for the delay. We're working on it. Your project is 'low priority.'"

Okay. I get that. I truly understand it.

In the context of all the pressing hospital business, I could grasp why our project was considered "low priority."

But still those words stung just a bit. For a few moments I felt small and unimportant.

Here is what I wonder:

Are our patients, as they await our own delayed phone calls, emails, and follow-ups (no doubt from our more pressing medical business), sometimes made to feel small and unimportant? Are they sometimes given the impression that they, too, are "low priority"?

DO THESE WORDS WORK?

I was waiting in line (one of my favorite pastimes) to register my complaint at some government bureaucracy. I won't go into the details of the situation but suffice it to say…they were wrong. I was right.

As I made my complaint (I guess you could say with a good deal of enthusiasm), the government bureaucrat (who shall, as always, remain nameless and faceless) said something that rocketed my usual cool, calm, and collected "waiting in line" demeanor (ha ha) to the stratosphere. (Now for the record I had made no threats of imminent harm to any government official nor had I threatened to incinerate any government building.)

Here is what Ms. Government Bureaucrat said:

"Sir," she chastised me, "Do not raise your voice in this office!"

Imagine yourself in my situation, frustrated and angry as I was.

How do you think these words made me feel?

Do you think those words made it likely I would lower my voice?

Would those words help a solution?

Perhaps we physicians and healers need to think about this when dealing with our own angry and frustrated customers. Now I am not saying it is okay to allow our patients to shout at us or abuse our staff.

All I'm saying is this:

Telling folks, "Do not raise your voice in this office," are words that may not work.

JARGON: WORDS THAT WORK

SHARON'S ANGEL

Several years ago my friend Sharon discovered a little "blemish," as she put it, on her breast. Upon evaluation by her surgeon, Dr. Susan Heckman, the "blemish" turned out to be nothing serious at all. But during the examination Dr. Heckman discovered in the other breast a suspicious lump. Dr. Heckman advised surgery.

However, Sharon believed in the power of holistic healing. Her belief was that cancer, like all physical ailments, could be overcome by the cosmic healing power of the psyche. Given her distrust of organized medicine, Sharon had her mind made up. She would defer surgery. For the next two months she would explore her own personal pathway to health.

She'd check out health food store curatives.

Possibly a session with Dr. Bernie Siegel.

Perhaps a séance with Deepak Chopra.

Maybe some fire walking with Tony Robbins.

If it doesn't work out in two months, Sharon told herself, *I'll come back to Dr. Heckman.*

But something was puzzling Sharon.

"By the way, Dr. Heckman," she asked upon leaving, "what exactly was that 'blemish' that brought me here in the first place?"

Now Dr. Susan Heckman could have said a lot of things.

We all have our packaged doctor spiels, medical mumbo-jargon that we love to spout, like...

"That 'blemish,' Sharon, was merely an epithelial lesion of no clinical import." or "That 'blemish,' Sharon, was a benign pigmented nevus with inconsequential mitotic potential."

We all know the drill.

But Dr. Susan Heckman knows how to listen to people, especially when those people happen to be her patients. So I suspect Dr. Heckman had some idea about the metaphysical ballpark in which Sharon went to bat. Instead of the usual doctor speak, here's what Dr. Heckman answered:

"Sharon," she smiled. "that 'blemish' was your guardian angel giving you a wake-up call."

At that moment everything changed. Sharon got it. She knew that Dr. Susan Heckman spoke her language. She knew Dr. Heckman understood. By the next morning surgery was completed. The diagnosis was cancer. But to this day, now many years later, my friend Sharon is free of disease.

Now did getting surgery two months earlier help Sharon beat breast cancer?

Maybe it did.

Maybe it didn't.

I choose to believe it did.

As a matter of fact, I would submit that it was Dr. Susan Heckman's skill as a communicator, as much as her expertise as a surgeon, that saved my friend Sharon's life.

Any doubters?

Just ask Sharon's angel.

HOW TO FEEL GOOD ABOUT BEING "STRESSED OUT"

"Stressed out," was the diagnosis I had given myself several years ago during a particular rough patch: overwork in a temporarily under-manned department, getting home late, volunteering Tuesday nights at the USO, attending my sons' soccer games, and fulfilling duties as board member of my synagogue. These were some of the culprits in the mix. I was feeling overwhelmed. And yes, I was feeling "stressed out."

Not only was it painful to be feeling "stressed out," but this diagnosis made me feel like a wimp. By gosh, I made it through medical school, internship, residency, fellowship, and even Miss Lottie Wilson's tenth grade Calculus class. Heck, once upon a time, I even memorized the Krebs Cycle! I thought I was made of tougher stuff. I confided all this to my colleague, Dr. Will North. Expecting a perfunctory confirmation of this "stressed out" self-diagnosis, instead, I was given a creative new way to look at things.

"No, Scott" said Will, "your problem is not that you are "stressed out."

Your problem," continued Will, "is that you are 'too passionate about life!"

"Wow," thought I, "Too passionate about life?"

I liked that.

For the first time in days, I think I smiled.

The shame of the label, "stressed out," was lifted.

My friends,

If some of you have been afflicted with the "stressed out" self-diagnosis,

If you too, because of this diagnosis, feel like a wimp,

Think again.

Perhaps you too, might be "too passionate about life."

GOT A RATTLE IN YOUR JALOPY?

Like many of you, my fellow physicians, I see a lot of folks with benign, harmless, but rather bizarre and not neatly diagnosable types of symptoms. In my field, neurology, lots of folks seem afflicted with what we call the "dizzies," the "tingles," or the "gurgles." Most of the time I haven't the faintest clue as to what is causing this stuff. And although I can't give it a specific diagnostic name, I try to reassure folks these symptoms are nothing serious. They are nothing to worry about, and they will very likely go away with time. You know the drill. Now many patients are okay with this, but some remain downright peeved because they don't get a specific diagnosis:

"My gosh, Edna, I plucked down twenty bucks for that visit, the least that so-called specialist could do is give me some answers!"

I get that.

Let's face it.

When folks visit the doctor they want the doctor to tell them what the heck is wrong.

Recently a colleague explained to me how she handles this situation. Here are the words she uses:

"So, Dwayne, I can't tell you exactly what's causing this tingle or twitch or gurgle in your body. But it's kind of like when you notice a little rattle in your car. Your expert mechanic checks it out. He listens to the rattle. He tells you he could do a lot of tests on this car, take it apart, fender to fender, and still never find that darn rattle. He would also tell you that he's heard a lot of rattles just like this one. He would reassure you that it was nothing serious, that it would be nothing to worry about, and that your engine won't conk out in the middle of the freeway.

"Well, Dwayne," continues my colleague, "that's about what we're dealing with here. You've got a little rattle in your own human body engine. Now I could do lots of X-rays and such. I could take you apart head to foot and I bet you I still couldn't find that darn rattle. But I can reassure you it's nothing serious, it's nothing to worry about. Your body's "engine" is not gonna conk out on you either."

Whatever we do for a living we all meet customers with whom there are no clear answers. Though their problem, we know, is not anything serious, not anything worth worrying about. Maybe it would help to give these folks a ride in a metaphorical jalopy.

JOY

A MOMENT OF EXQUISITE JOY

Our son Jeremy, at age nineteen, one night had excruciating abdominal pain and unrelenting vomiting. We brought him to the hospital. His intestines were blocked. We feared he would need emergency surgery. But after three days of hospital treatment with IV fluids and nasogastric tube decompression, Jeremy recovered. As a matter of fact, I joyously recall the exact moment of his recovery. My wife and I, who had spent three hospital cot nights at Jeremy's bedside, just about did a celebratory pole dance on the IV stand at that moment, the moment we had been praying for, the moment when our son Jeremy…first passed gas!

Who knew such joyous exhilaration could come from a simple fart?

LEADERSHIP

LEADERSHIP: THE DEFINITION

What makes a good leader? (Please read no further until you have formulated an answer.)

I bet most folks answered by listing specific leadership qualities, such as charisma, boldness, availability, compassion, insight, energy, vision, courage, communication skill, etc. Though these qualities, no doubt, may be important for leadership, let's try to look at leadership from a different perspective. Let's try to look at it from a backwards perspective. Let's try to reverse engineer the definition.

In other words, what is the effect of the leader? What is the result of that leader's leadership? How will that leader's team, and individuals on that team, be inspired to act.

Let me try to explain this further. Do you remember the movie "As Good as It Gets?" The main character, Melvin Udall, (Jack Nicholson) is afflicted by extreme OCD. Melvin insults everyone he meets. No one can stand to be around him. He hates medicines. And even though medication would help his condition, Melvin refuses to take it.

However, in a memorable scene near the end of the movie, he confesses to Carol, (Helen Hunt) the only waitress in the diner who can tolerate serving him, that he has begun taking the detested medication. And in that confession, he reveals the "backwards," "reverse engineered" definition of a leader: "You make me," he tells Carol, "want to be a better man."

And that is what a leader does, is it not? Perhaps the definition of leadership is less about the qualities a leader possesses, and more about the **effect** the leader inspires. Like Carol, a true leader must inspire a life change.

I am grateful that my own life has been blessed by several such leaders, leaders who have made me, want to be a better man.

STEP INTO MY OFFICE

Within our medical group I know of a particular department chief. Periodically "The Chief" summons one of his doctors to step into his private office. Here is what "The Chief" says:

"Dr. Jones, I've got no negative Physician Satisfaction survey scores to give you today. There are no patient complaint letters this week. There are no medical-legal cases pending against you. I called you in today because I want to tell you something important. You, Dr. Jones, are doing one helluva job! Thank you."

End of conversation.

End of meeting.

Something to consider:

How often do we ask folks under our supervision, to "Step into my office?

All of us are "The Chief" to someone.

THE POWER OF
LISTENING

THE MOST WONDERFUL COMPLIMENT I EVER RECEIVED

I saw a fellow in my neurology clinic with a long history of industrial injury and chronic pain. Over the years Michael had had his fill of doctors. I was not especially looking forward to our encounter. After looking over his long, complicated medical record before our appointment, I doubted there was anything I could do to help him.

But it turned out he was a very interesting guy. His mother and father, he told me, both worked on the Oakland docks as longshoremen. He, himself, was volunteering in the Oakland inner city neighborhoods, working with at risk, violent youth.

In truth I enjoyed his stories.

And while engrossed in the listening, I quietly managed to complete my neurological examination.

At the end of the visit I explained (surprise, surprise) that there was nothing much I could do to help him.

Michael didn't seem too upset by this.

As a matter of fact, he said he enjoyed the consultation with me.

Then he laid on me, perhaps the most wonderful compliment I have ever received in forty years of my physician life.

"Doc," he smiled. "you don't talk like a doctor. You talk like a normal person."

I thought more about this.

Perhaps the secret of *talking* like a 'normal' person…is to *listen* like one.

HOW TO CONVINCE YOUR PATIENTS (CUSTOMERS) THAT YOU ARE BRILLIANT

My father was a salesman. Yet in spite of his profession, Dad was not a talkative person. When Dad met a customer, his typical greeting was something like this: "So what's new, Joe?"

That was his sales pitch. Then Joe would proceed to tell what was new. Dad would listen. He would smile. He would nod his head and chuckle softly as he reached out to gently touch Joe's shoulder. But Dad would speak very little. And even though Dad was a quiet guy, his customers liked him. Many were counted as his friends.

Dad lived to be 101 years old. When he was in his late nineties his memory began failing. A lot of days he thought he was in Miss Dean's fifth-grade class at the Sherman Elementary School. When I visited my parents' home in Atlanta around this time, I drove my mother and father to their monthly senior citizen current events class at Emory University. Though Dad understood very little of what was said, after the lecture he strode up to the podium to give the Emory professor his customary thank-you.

I noted the professor then began speaking to Dad, and as he did so, the professor became more and more animated. Although Dad's memory had dimmed, his old personality flickered. Dad nodded, he smiled, he chuckled softly as he gently touched the professor's shoulder. But true to his nature, Dad spoke very little. After a time I approached the two. As I led Dad away the Emory professor turned to me, glanced toward my father, and announced: "That man is brilliant!"

And you know he is right.
My dad is brilliant.
He is brilliant because he knows the secret.
And the secret is this:
Let folks speak.
Listen.
We all know the power of the "spoken word."
Perhaps even more potent is the power of the "listened to word."
"So what's new, Joe?"

THE ONLY ACRONYM WORTH REMEMBERING

I hate acronyms. I hate them because N... R... A. (This has nothing to do with the second amendment.) N.R.A. translates in my mind to "Nobody Remembers Acronyms!" But there is one acronym I love. It is the only one I have ever found to be useful. It is the only one I ever thought worth remembering.

The acronym is... *WAIT: W... A... I... T.* Here's what it means:

Suppose you are talking to a patient, giving them your well-rehearsed-five-minute-educational spiel on one of those things you love to talk about. Or perhaps you are advising a colleague or making comments at meetings or conferences or even speaking with friends or family. Ever notice your listener's eyes glaze over? Ever think rather than speaking it would be more valuable for you to listen? Ever realize you have talked just too darn much? After the encounter ever wish, in fact, you had not spoken at all? Ever wish you had just...*shut up*?

That is why I love this acronym.

Before we speak, think:

W... A... I... T.

"Why... Am... I... Talking?"

Before we open our mouth, think:

W... A... I... T.

"Why... Am... I... Talking?"

I now have that acronym tattooed on my tongue!

MOM, ARE YOU LISTENING?

Mitch Albom in his book, *Have a Little Faith*, tells this story:

A little girl approaches her mother, as mom is preparing dinner.

"Mom," the little girl says with excitement, "guess what happened at school today?"

"What happened, honey?" says Mom, as she continues making tonight's casserole.

"Mom," the little girl continues, "You are not listening!"

Mom starts mixing the salad and, without a glance back at her daughter, answers, "What happened, sweetie? I'm listening."

"Mom," the little girl scolds, "You're not listening with your eyes!"

As physicians and healers, in the age where our electronic medical record screen has become our all-powerful focus, I wonder how many of our patients are (silently) scolding us...

"Doctor, you're not listening with your eyes!"

Personal note:

Whenever I write one of these columns I always ask my wife for her opinion.

Here is her comment about this one:

"Honey," she smiled. "in all the years of our marriage you have also been married to Kaiser Permanente. I know how that little girl feels."

THE POWER OF *LISTENING* AND ASKING THE RIGHT QUESTION

"HOW CAN I MAKE THINGS EASIER FOR YOU?"

Angela Serpa is a nurse practitioner who works in perioperative medicine. Several days before the scheduled surgery she telephones patients, making sure they understand all the particular details of their upcoming procedure. At the end of the phone visit, knowing that most folks find surgery a very frightening prospect, Angela always asks this question: "How can I make things easier for you?"

After asking this question to one such pre-operative patient, there occurred a long pause on the other line.

Finally, a voice answered, "You just did."

Author's Commentary

Here is, I believe, the communication lesson:

When we ask our patients about their perspective on their illness, when we ask them directly about their own concerns and worries, it can be a powerful way to build connection.

It can be a powerful way to build trust.

But sometimes what matters is not what our patients give in answer.

Sometimes what matters is simply that we ask the question.

PLAY BALL!

While I was treating one of my patients, my head nurse, Robyn, banged on my exam room door. "You better get your butt out in the waiting room, Abramson," she barked. "Your 2:40 consult is going berserk out there!"

I quickly excused myself from my current patient. My next patient, a guy about forty-five years old, wearing a Ford Motor Company hat, was shouting in front of our full waiting room.

"I ain't waitin'. I'm losin' money!"

"I ain't waitin'. I'm losin' money!"

I explained to the guy I was running late. I told him it would be about forty minutes.

"I ain't waitin'. I'm losin' money!" was the response.

I made a counteroffer. "Okay. How about thirty minutes?"

"I ain't waitin'; I'm losin' money!" was the repeated refrain.

I couldn't believe this. Here I was, a Kaiser health care professional. A real doctor. A specialist, mind you. And in front of a waiting room full of patients, I'm dickering with a lunatic! Finally...we made a deal...twenty minutes, and he agreed to shut up.

We then faced off in the exam room. Believe me, I was about as thrilled to see him as he was to see me. But I dutifully went through my neurology routine. This parts manager from the local Ford dealership had long time back pain. Now, in spite of the pain, Mr. Ford Parts didn't want time off work. He didn't want narcotics. He didn't want to file a lawsuit against his boss. (I hate to sound cynical, but I began to wonder what the heck he did want.)

Now here is where my communication training came in handy. Although I'm still fuming from our waiting room battle, I figure I

122

might as well put the training to use; I figure I'll try the "patient perspective" habit.

"So Mr. Ford Motor Guy," I hiss through my gritted teeth, "tell me, Sir,"—as I search my bag of "getting patient perspective" questions—"What is the worst thing about your pain?" (Seeing as how he didn't want drugs, a job excuse, or a lawyer evaluation, it seemed like a pretty good "patient perspective" question to ask.)

He thought for a moment. Then, for the first time, he looked directly at me. "I have a twelve-year-old son," he replied, "and I can't play catch with him."

Wham!

I got it.

I connected.

At the time this encounter occurred, my own son was about that age. A few years earlier I had had a pinched nerve in my arm. I too feared I might not be able to ever play catch again with my son. I told Mr. Ford Guy my story. He nodded his head.

Just like that, the whole atmosphere in the room changed.

We talked about baseball.

We talked about playing catch with our sons.

I am not going to tell you I cured his chronic back pain. My point is not to say good communication skills lead to cures for angry, frustrated patients. Sometimes they do. Most times they don't. But what did happen here was getting the patient perspective, asking the right question, asking specifically what the worst thing about the pain was. And I believe by asking that question, an angry, confrontational medical visit was transformed into a meaningful connection between two human beings who happened to be fathers to baseball-catching sons.

As physicians and healers, sometimes it is more important to find out, not "what's the matter?" But finding out "what matters."

And when we ask the right questions, when we "get in the game," sometimes we might even hit a home run.

"IT'S NOT MY POSITION"

Amber was referred to me for a routine neurological problem. She had told my receptionist she was apprehensive about seeing doctors. As I entered the exam room she seemed unsettled, uncomfortable. The feeling was palpable and before I began my evaluation, I asked her why she seemed so reluctant to have come for this visit.

"Last year," she began, "after the birth of my son, I was having a medical problem. I went to my doctor. She examined me. She told me I had diagnosis 'X.' She gave me medication for diagnosis 'X.' But when I heard all this it did not quite make sense to me. I really did not think I had diagnosis X. However I thought to myself: *She's the doctor. To question her medical judgment, it is not my position.*"

"So I took the medicine for a month," she continued, "just like my doctor told me to. I felt worse. Finally after numerous phone calls and a consultation with another doctor, they figured out what was really wrong. But I suffered for a month. And I put into my body unnecessary medicine. And deep down I knew I was given the wrong diagnosis."

Now when I heard this story, here is what I thought.

What if this doctor had asked a few simple questions? Like...

"Does diagnosis 'X' seem right to you?" or "How would you feel about taking medication for diagnosis 'X'?" or simply "Do you have any more concerns about what I have discussed with you today?"

And here is a question to all of us clinicians and healers:

How many of our patients have sat in our exam rooms silently thinking, "It's not my position..."

"HEAD 'EM OFF AT THE PASS"

My wife had a viral respiratory infection. Her doctor patiently explained about viral infections. He told her it was not necessary to take antibiotics. He said antibiotics sometimes could be harmful. Pamela asked me my opinion. I told her I agreed completely with her doctor's advice. But Pamela still seemed unsettled.

When we got home she called her mother. Now Pamela's mother is a wonderful woman. I love her dearly. However she is not a Johns Hopkins professor. She was a lifelong seamstress with a tenth-grade education. But Mom was emphatic. She told her daughter to hightail it back to the doctor and get herself antibiotics. Pronto.

Okay. Now at this point Pamela had three opinions on her viral respiratory illness.

Her own doctor advised no antibiotics.

Her husband, the doctor, advised no antibiotics.

Her mother, the seamstress, advised exactly the opposite.

So whose advice did Pamela take?

(Okay. It's a trick question. We all know when it comes to advice from mothers-in-law…there are no other options.)

Yep. So quicker than you could say, "Hi Ho, Silver!" Pamela galloped back to the doctor's office, demanding antibiotics.

Here is the point: When we see our patients even when we see them one-to-one, we do not see them in isolation. They come with a lot of gear stuffed in the saddle bag. In other words we've got competition.

The Internet

Dr. Dean Edell

The National Enquirer

Aunt Bertha

My mother-in-law

Sometimes our competitors are in the exam room with us; often times they are on the outside of it. But they are a powerful force. They are tough hombres. And if we ignore them, if we don't give them their "props," they may stampede us every time.

So what could have been done differently? In this case probably not much.

But consider this:

How about we ask our patients about these competitive forces?

What if we lasso all these background concerns and corral them in at the get-go?

Why not get all the cards on the table?

So while our patients are still in the exam room, why not pop these questions?

What information have you researched off the internet?

What have you heard Dr. Dean Edell say?

What's the latest scoop you've read in the National Enquirer?

What does Aunt Bertha think?

Let's have our showdown with the competition right up front.

Let's beat them to the draw.

Like John Wayne, let's "head 'em off at the pass!"

And who knows?

We might even have a fighting chance against my mother-in-law. Giddyup!

THE MOST UNUSUAL CAUSE FOR DIZZINESS

A Filipino gentleman visited my neurology clinic accompanied by his pregnant wife. Mr. Ramos was referred for dizziness. There had been other clinic visits with numerous other physicians for the same problem. All examinations were normal. All tests were negative. The consensus was that he had that vague, benign, nonspecific nothing-really-wrong-with-you kind of dizziness. But the explanations by other doctors seemed not to satisfy. Hence this appointment for consultation with me in the neurology clinic.

My evaluation was no different. I was about to launch into my own five-minute version of the nothing-wrong-with-you dizziness diagnosis when I realized I'd probably be just as unsuccessful as the other doctors.

So I figured I'd try out the getting-the-patient's-perspective approach. There was not much to lose. I asked Mr. Ramos what he, himself, thought might be causing the dizziness.

"Don't know, Doc," he shrugged. "That's why they sent me to see you."

Okay. Strike one on "getting patient perspective."

But I was ready for the next pitch. Since "getting patient perspective" means also getting perspective of significant others. I turned to Mrs. Ramos, asking what she thought might be making her husband dizzy. She seemed to have the answer.

"Well, Doc," she explained, "with my first two kids I was very sick…nausea, vomiting, dizziness, the morning sickness every day. Now I'm pregnant with my third. I feel fine. I believe my husband is experiencing my morning sickness; it is afflicting him. What do you think, Doc?"

I turned to Mr. Ramos. Nodding in assent, he added sheepishly, "It's possible, isn't it, Doc?"

Now I could have spent the next five minutes debunking their superstitious beliefs and presenting my own brilliant explanation of the nothing-wrong-with-you dizziness syndrome. Instead I decided to invoke the words of one of my old medical school professors. These three magical words have helped me out of a lot of tight spots.

"Mr. Ramos," I continued thoughtfully, "as for suffering from the 'Pregnant Husband Morning Sickness Dizziness Syndrome,' well…let me tell you,"—and now those three magic words—"We see that."

They both smiled in agreement.

That was it.

They now had their answer.

Their concerns were validated.

End of visit.

No need for more consultations.

No need for the five-minutes nothing-wrong-with-you dizziness spiel.

They were happy.

I was happy.

Asking "patient perspective" saved my day.

Postscript: I thought this story so amusing I recounted it to my wife over dinner that night. Pamela didn't think it was funny.

"Now let's just hope," my wife intoned darkly, "he'll get the labor pains too."

THE POWER OF *LISTENING*

(There May Be an Exception to Every Rule)

"DID YOUR PROVIDER INVOLVE YOU IN MEDICAL DECISION-MAKING?"

I went to the optometry department to pick up some new glasses. The optometry technician asked what type of glasses I wanted. I had no idea what was the 'in' style.

"Just pick me out a pair," I said, "that will make me look cool and good."

But the technician, ignoring my request, showed me one frame after another. She kept asking which I preferred. Truth is I had no idea what I preferred. All I wanted was to look sporty. I was getting real frustrated telling her again and again to give me something real snazzy.

Now I realize nowadays we are supposed to champion "patient-centered health care," which means giving the patient a large part of the power to choose their health care path. Gone are the days of the all-knowing, authoritarian physician. We label ourselves now as "health care providers." One of the Patient Satisfaction Survey questions that we are graded on is "Did 'provider' involve you in medical decision-making?"

But doggone it, like with my glasses, I just wanted my 'provider' to make the decision. I figured she knew more than me about making an old geezer look spiffy. I wanted her to tell me what to do.

I wonder if our patients sometimes want that too.

MISCELLANEOUS LESSONS OF LIFE

THE BEST ADVICE I EVER GAVE

As a neurologist, I see lots of folks sent from the ER with spells of fainting. Sometimes it's hard to know whether this was a simple faint or an actual seizure, since when folks faint occasionally their bodies can stiffen or jerk briefly. It can sometimes be difficult to make the correct diagnosis. What I have found most fruitful as I consult is to inquire about what happened in one's life the day of the event.

Recently I saw a young woman, along with her husband, with such a spell. Here is what happened in her life the day of this simple faint versus epileptic seizure:

That morning her newlywed husband was playing softball with the guys. Later, as she drove to meet him at the Olive Garden restaurant, she texted him. She asked if he missed her.

Texting back, he answered, "No."

"I was so angry at dinner," she said, "that I could not eat. I could not even speak. Then I passed out."

As I said, getting lifestyle information on the day of the event can come in handy. In this case it clearly led to a diagnosis of a simple fainting spell and not anything as serious as epilepsy.

Now I am not a judgmental person.

Okay. Let me amend that.

I am judgmental but I usually hide it pretty well.

But this time I could not hold back.

I turned to the young husband.

"You have got to be," I gently admonished, "dumber than a damn goat."

He silently nodded in agreement.

"Next time," I said, "when your bride asks if you missed her, you will say what?"

(I made him fill in the blank.)

And that, I believe, in over forty years of neurology practice, is the best advice I ever gave.

Addendum: The prince and his princess bride lived happily ever after.

(Maybe.)

JUDGED IN OUR WEAKEST MOMENT

Vignette No. 1

One of our ER doctors told me about a patient who registered a complaint about his care. The patient was an Eastern European whose name was chock full of letters like C, J, K, and Z. As he approached the bedside the doctor picked up the chart, looked at the patient, glanced back at the chart, then said the words that engendered the complaint:

"May I," asked the doctor, "buy a vowel?" The doctor thought it was funny. The patient and his family did not. And even though the overall care was excellent (perhaps even lifesaving), still a letter of complaint was written. Bottom line: What happened here is that the physician was judged not by his overall medical care but by his weakest moment.

Vignette No. 2

My friend Anne recently attended one of those "change your life" seminars.

The trainer asked how many folks were parents.

Most raised their hands.

The trainer asked how many thought they were, overall, fairly good parents.

Most raised their hands.

The trainer asked how many thought they might have at least one area of weakness as a parent.

Most raised their hands.

"Okay," said the trainer, "how would you like it if your own kids judged you only on the weakest part of your parenting?"

Sometimes, as clinicians and healers, it's the little things that screw us up.

"Doctor didn't apologize for being late."

"Doctor forgot my first name."

"Doctor made a tacky joke."

It may not be fair but in medicine, as in parenting, often times we're judged by our weakest moments.

Postscript: After the seminar my friend Anne (who had had some longtime issues with her own mother) decided to call her long-distance. Anne thanked her mother…for having been her mom. On a phone line two thousand miles away, there was a pause that seemed to last forever.

"You will never know," Mom finally answered, "how long I've been waiting for this call."

TAKE ANOTHER LOOK AT YOUR CHILD'S BABY PICTURES

I attended a lecture by a very prominent child psychiatrist. To be honest though, I forgot a lot about what he said. But there was one thing from that lecture that I remember to this day. His fifteen-year-old son, he told us, did not seem to have much aptitude for schoolwork. No matter how much this brilliant psychiatrist father encouraged him, the boy did not have much desire to even try to do the schoolwork. He was barely getting by with C's and D's.

The doctor father was disappointed in his son's academic performance. And if truth be told, he was disappointed in his son. He did not envision this in his offspring. One day, perhaps by chance, he began looking at his son's baby pictures. It reminded him of how much he loved his son. It also reminded him of how much academic performance had become the measure of his son's acceptance. He sent a letter to his son. He wrote only these words: "I love you."

I heard this. My own son was having difficulties in high school. I looked at his baby pictures once again. I wrote him an email. I didn't write the usual stuff about getting good grades, about working hard, or about thinking of the future.

In the email I wrote only these words: "I love you."

So here's a suggestion:

If your own kids perhaps have not won a Nobel Prize or a gold medal in the Olympics or perhaps maybe just not turning out exactly like you expected, why not take another look at their baby pictures?

Addendum: After my son received this "I love you" email, guess what he answered?

His exact response:

"Dad," he asked, "are you alright?"

TATS ARE FOREVER

As I prepared a young woman in my exam room for a routine spinal tap, as is my usual practice, I asked her boyfriend to remain in the waiting area. During the procedure, I could not help but notice the woman had a large heart tattooed on her derriere. Inside the heart were the words "Dwayne Forever."

After the procedure I went back to the waiting area.

"Dwayne," I said, "Wanda did just fine. You can go back to join her now."

The guy did not give me a happy look.

"My name," he scowled, "is not Dwayne!"

The moral of the story?

In life, unlike tattoos, nothing is forever.

Addendum: Okay. With dermatological procedures I realize one can erase tattoos. But I think there is still a message here. And besides, how else could I share with you the romantic saga of Wanda and Dwayne?

DON'T WISH ME "GOOD LUCK"

Brandon is a very polite and well-mannered, young man. He also happens to be a professional mixed martial arts fighter. About every six months Brandon shows up in my clinic with a State of California Athletic Commission form that I must fill out to certify he is cleared neurologically to ply his trade. Once, as he was leaving my office, forms completed for his upcoming fight, I wished him "Good luck."

"Don't wish me luck, Doc." Brandon turned around to answer. "Luck is for those who don't prepare. Wish me 'Good Execution.'"

I think Brandon is on to something. Think about it: If one needs "luck" to succeed, what does this say about their desire to prepare, to work hard, to overcome obstacles, to succeed in whatever mission they choose? In fact, come to think of it, if you wish someone "Good luck," it may well be an insult.

HOW TO RAISE SUCCESSFUL AND DECENT CHILDREN

Dr. Elaine Ong got married on May 3, 2008. One of our pediatricians at Kaiser Hayward, Elaine is one of four siblings who are all physicians. Not only are Elaine and her sisters and brother top notch doctors, but all are notably musically accomplished. Elaine herself is a concert-level violinist. But more than this, knowing Elaine, one cannot fail to be impressed by her cheerfulness, modesty, and downright decency.

Elaine's parents were immigrants from China. Sam Ong, her dad, when he arrived in America as a young man, spoke no English. He went to night school to learn the language. He eventually worked for thirty years as a pharmacist for Thrifty Drug Store. Elaine's mom, Peggy, a housewife, later went back to school also and then became a grammar school teacher. For the many years I have known Elaine, I had secretly marveled at the Ong family story. Being a father myself, I was curious about how Sam and Peggy raised such successful and decent kids. I wondered what secrets of child rearing they held.

I was invited to the wedding. At the dinner reception I sat next to a very distinguished gentleman, Dr. Warren Van Bronkhorst, who had been Elaine's violin teacher. Warren said Sam would "schlep" (it's an old Chinese word) all four Ong kids, one after the other, thirty-five miles from their home in Sacramento to his music studio in Stockton. He said Sam was a tough taskmaster.

"You know," he mused, "in my profession I have seen that kind of pressure break a lot of kids. But the Ong family seemed to thrive on it. They happily got stronger and stronger."

I could not wait to meet Sam. I had so many things I wanted to ask. Finally, as the bridal party made their way to visit the tables, I got my chance. As Sam approached I leaped to my feet. But alas, as I shook his hand, all I heard myself blurt out was "Sam, you are my hero!"

Then I calmed down a bit, recovered my composure, and asked him the question I had pondered for years: "Sam what is the secret," I pleaded, "how do you raise such successful and decent kids?"

Sam didn't answer the question. He glanced over at Warren Van Bronkhorst, the former piano teacher, and smiled. Turning back to me this is what he said:

"We also invited Elaine's grammar school principal but he couldn't come. Those who give you a helping hand," he continued, "you never forget."

Then Sam moved on to greet Dr. Van Bronkhorst and the other guests.

I thought about Sam's words.

Maybe he answered the question after all.

RETIREMENT

THE STARBUCKS HUSTLE
A RETIREMENT REFLECTION

I'm heading into Starbucks for my morning coffee fix. About twenty paces from me, almost equidistant from the entrance, I see a young woman walking toward it with the same intention as myself. I figure one more person in the line could mean a delay of approximately fifty-six seconds. So I begin to hurry my step (not in any obvious, tacky way of course), but *I know I need to get there first.*

Then I realize this fact: I retired thirteen days ago. There is no need to rush anywhere. I relax for a moment, feeling relief about my new status in the ranks of the unemployed and the unhurried. But alas, I cannot help myself. I break into a slow trot. Again, not too obvious. I try to be subtle, more like I'm just trying to keep in shape with a mild jog step. But I refuse to lose fifty-six seconds from my life. I am not gonna let this sucker beat me to the coffee line in Starbucks!

There is an old saying:

"A doctor is ready to retire when they no longer need to be called 'doctor.'"

Maybe there is truth in that.

But by the same token, maybe a doctor is ready to retire when they no longer need to engage in the Starbucks' hustle.

Here's hoping that may happen to me down the road, many lattes from now.

THE ONE CONSTANT

I ran into one of our retired Kaiser Permanente doctors. He had worked for Kaiser for over thirty years. I asked him if he missed practicing medicine.

"Not really," he replied. "But I'll tell you what I do miss. During my thirty years in the organization I had my own personal health concerns. I had three marriages and two divorces. I had problems with kids, grandkids, and stepkids. I had issues with mothers-in-law. But the one constant for me in all those years…was my work. And what I miss most about work is the morning chats over coffee with my colleagues. I miss the kibitzing about patients, politics, or ex-wives. That's what I miss about practicing medicine. I miss the fellowship. I miss the friends."

Someday, when all of us look back on our own careers, what we too may miss are those same morning chats over coffee with colleagues. What we may miss, above all else, is each other. And as our day-to-day professional lives roll on, perhaps it is that special physician camaraderie that we need to honor.

SALESMANSHIP

THE SECRET OF SELLING ANYTHING (INCLUDING MEDICAL ADVICE)

One of my young patients had recently graduated from a small liberal arts college in Ohio, majoring in English Literature. Daniel had moved back home to the San Francisco Bay Area to live with his parents. With that kind of college background, I asked him if it had been difficult to find a job. Daniel agreed it was. He said most college grads with a major like his had two job choices: sales or Starbucks. He chose sales. He took a job selling some sort of software business program. Eight hours a day, he cold called strangers. Although Daniel never envisioned this as his career path, he was making some good money.

I am fascinated by those in the sales industry. (Maybe it's because in a way, every day with every patient, we physicians are selling something: maybe a new cholesterol medication or a referral to stop smoking program or most important of all, trust in our competence.)

I asked Daniel the secret of being successful in sales.

Without missing a beat, Daniel answered, "It's not about selling the product, it's about selling yourself."

I loved his response.

Then I asked the inevitable follow-up question: "So then," I inquired, "how do you sell yourself?"

To me, no matter what we do for a living, this is one of life's ultimate questions.

Before I reveal his response, let's think about this question.

How would we personally answer it?

How would we sell ourselves?

(Please read no further till an answer comes to mind.)

His response to this question I loved even more.

"How do I sell myself?" Daniel repeated, "It's simple. I listen. I listen to my customers."

Maybe there's a lesson here for all of us physician salesmen.

GREAT ADVICE FROM A DOOR-TO-DOOR MAGAZINE SELLER

Glenda, one of my neurology clinic patients, had grown up in the projects of Baltimore. At age fifteen, she set out into the world. She hooked up with a door-to-door magazine sales company, traveling all over America with their crews. She said she made a good living. I was fascinated. Most folks look upon these people as pushy intruders, as annoyances, as doorbell-ringing pests. I know this to be a truth because in my high school years, I also tried to sell magazines door-to-door. I was terrible at it. I could not sell squat. I was curious about Glenda's success. So I asked her the secret of selling.

"I never give people the phony line," she said, "that I'm trying to earn money for college. That's hogwash. I never tell them I'm trying to send orphans to summer camp. That's bulls——. But what I do is simply this: I look at them directly. I smile. And then I say these words: 'Ma'am, may I take a moment of your time? *I have something that will make your life better.*'"

All this got me thinking.

We all have those patients who just don't want to pay attention to our healing advice. Perhaps they look on us as annoyances, as pests, as... well...doorbell-ringing magazine salesmen. And whether it's diabetic management, referral to stop smoking clinic, or a healthy eating hand-out, maybe we can take a page from Glenda's magazine-selling playbook.

Perhaps, like Glenda, we might look folks directly in the eye, smile, and utter the simple words of a door-to-door magazine salesman:

"Ma'am, may I take a moment of your time? *I have something that will make your life better.*"

"I'M DAMN GOOD!"

Reggie Jackson was a hall of fame baseball player. Because of his talent for hitting home runs in the playoffs and World Series, he was called, "Mr. October." Reggie's score on his own ego-meter, it was said, even surpassed his batting average. He was a promoter's dream. They even marketed a candy bar, "the Reggie Bar," after him.

"When you unwrap the candy," remarked his teammate Jim Catfish Hunter, "*it* tells *you* how good it is!"

Now maybe there's a communication lesson here for us physicians. Maybe, just a little, we need to toot our own horn, blow our own whistle, sing our own praises. I realize this is not what we learned in Sunday school, but consider this scenario: We have just told our patient about a procedure we will perform on them. We dutifully lay out the benefits and explain the risks. We could leave it at that, or we could add…

"George, let me tell you one more thing. I've done hundreds of these. I have great confidence in my ability. You could not be in better hands. Count on it. I am damn good!"

Maybe, like Mr. October's candy bar, we need to let folks know just how good we are.

Perhaps we need to let our patients know we hit home runs, not just in October, but in every month of the year.

THE POWER OF THE PERSONAL

I was in Staples office supply store shopping for a laptop computer for my wife. The salesman seemed very knowledgeable. He showed me several computers, describing the capability and the specifications of each. Frankly I understood very little of what he said (though in these situations, I always try to look as comprehending as I can). So after each laptop spiel, I found myself giving him the "knowing nod," but truth be told, I had no idea what he was talking about. And I still had no idea what to buy for Pamela. Then as he showed me one more computer, he uttered the following statement:

"I bought this one for my sister."

That did it.

Those words sealed the deal.

I needed to know nothing else.

If he bought this model for his own sister...

How could I not trust his judgment?

I bought the computer.

As physicians (or whatever we do for a living), maybe there is a lesson here for us.

Sometimes sharing our personal lives can build trust with those who seek our help.

"Yes, Ms. Jones, my wife had those same symptoms. She took the same medicine. She's doing fine now. This medicine could help you too."

Sometimes, in communication challenges, personal experience can trump technical expertise.

Sometimes, as with my Staples' salesman, what seals the deal is...

"The Power of the Personal."

THE BUSINESS
OF MEDICINE

"YOU HAVE A CHOICE OF AIRLINES"

"We know you have a choice of airlines. Thank you for choosing United."

As my plane landed, those familiar words were pronounced over the loudspeaker. I'm sure you folks have heard the same generic announcement. But it got me thinking. What if United were, in fact, *the* only airline company? What if we did not have a choice of airlines? What if there were no competition? Would United Airlines thank us for choosing them? Would they really care how their customers rate them?

On the other hand what if other organizations, like the DMV for example, did, in fact, have competition? Wouldn't it be great to hear the following announcement: "Thank you for choosing the DMV to get your driver's license. We know you have a choice of companies out there from which to get your license. Thank you for choosing us."

Let me put this another way. When was the last time a DMV bureaucrat employee thanked you for your business?

Here is the point: When there is no competition, why would the DMV (or any organization) care about what customers think? Why would they strive for better service? Heck, they know we'll be coming back no matter what.

And what if health care provider companies had no competition?

Would we be like the DMV?

Would we care about what our "customers" think?

I, for one, am glad we have a competitive health care provider system.

I think it makes the medical profession better.

I think it makes us step up our game.

We have to earn our customers' trust.

NEXT TIME YOU HIRE A PHYSICIAN...

Dr. Chitra Reddy, our chief of nephrology, after fifteen years of service to Kaiser Hayward transferred to Kaiser Santa Clara. One of her final duties was to choose a successor chief. Now of course all the applicants came with top notch credentials, glowing recommendations from supervisors and exams that were aced in every test since middle school.

It was a daunting task to choose among so many highly qualified applicants.

Dr. Reddy, however, is a woman of common-sense wisdom.

She knew she must ask the one person who would know the most about the potential candidates. She knew she must ask...the department receptionist.

"So tell me, Rita," Dr. Reddy asked the receptionist, "what were these doctors like when they came for the interview?"

"Oh, some were so nice," said reception clerk Rita, "but some were so rude. They would break in line and demand to be escorted to Dr. Reddy's office STAT."

Guess which ones did not get the job?

Dr. Reddy understood the definition of "grace." Grace is not about how we treat our chiefs. It is not even about how we treat our peers and colleagues. But it is everything about how we treat those whose station we perceive beneath us.

Next time you hire anybody, ask the person who may know best: Ask the security guard, the cleaning lady, or reception clerk Rita.

MY AMAZING ADVENTURE INTO THE FEE FOR SERVICE WORLD (AND INTO THE HOME PAGE OF DR. JEFF SOBEL)

My entire professional career, over forty years, I have worked in the Kaiser Permanente world. A few months ago, I slipped my toes into the murky waters of the "Fee for Service World." One of my patients needed a special medication form approved by an outside contractor.

I spoke to a very sweet person by the name of Amber. But after talking with her for thirteen minutes and twenty-three seconds and after telling her five times, finally Amber realized I was the "doctor" and not the "patient." (Though throughout the entire conversation, she persisted in calling me, "Scott.")

I will not go into how many times I had to spell my name, spell the patient's name, give my date of birth, the patient's date of birth, various addresses, phone numbers, and the last four digits of this or that. Finally Amber informed me she had all the information she needed. She asked if I would mind waiting two minutes while she confirmed the information with her supervisor.

I replied that I would very much "mind waiting." I said that I was, in fact, very angry about waiting. I informed her I was a busy doctor. Furthermore I told her I considered this entire conversation a waste of my precious doctor time. And besides, I said, there were only so many crossword puzzles I could do while waiting for her supervisor.

155

Anyway about three crossword puzzles later (it was not two minutes but seven minutes and thirty-seven seconds later…but who was counting?), Amber came back on the line.

Always maintaining her sweet demeanor, Amber informed me that my patient's request had been denied. But then, helpful as always, she asked if I'd like to learn how to appeal the decision.

I told Amber she was probably a decent and good person. I told her I was a grumpy old person. But I figured listening to how to appeal the decision would take another four or five crossword puzzles. I hung up the phone.

Now this was one of those bad hair days for me. However only for a few moments that day did the "fee for service" bureaucratic waters nip at my own toes. I have "fee for service" world physician friends who every day spend hours in those same waters up to their umbilicus.

Now what does this have to do with the home page of Kaiser cardiologist Dr. Jeff Sobel? In his home page introduction of himself to his patients, Dr. Sobel summarized succinctly the Kaiser mission:

"The reason I joined Kaiser Permanente," wrote Dr. Sobel, "was because I wanted to practice effective medicine…not effective billing."

I hear you, Dr. Jeff Sobel. And I am grateful to Kaiser Permanente for this: for most of my day, I, too, get to practice "effective medicine, not effective billing." And for most of my day, I don't have to do crossword puzzles awaiting medication approval from the likes of Miss Amber. (Even though she is probably a decent and sweet person.)

THE "UPSELL"

Does this scenario sound familiar? You bring your car into the dealership for just a routine servicing. The service representative (patch on his shirt says his name is "Bob") checks your car history. He tells you they will do the routine service check, but he also recommends the "manifold inspection," a "carburetor cleaning," and a "transmission flush." Now you have no idea what the hell a manifold is or does, but you don't want Bob to think you are an automobile maintenance moron. So you give a pseudo-knowing nod as you sheepishly agree to the "new and improved" service plan.

Dear Reader: you have just been suckered into what Bob and his ilk call, "The Upsell."

I myself know nothing about carburetors, transmissions, or manifolds. But one of my patients, who happens to be a service manager in this business, has confessed to me that all these things, in most instances, are totally unnecessary.

But it is a "win…win…win" situation for everybody.

The dealership makes more money.

Bob makes a bigger commission.

The customer thinks he is getting his car in extra tip-top shape.

And all this got me thinking. In our medical business are we not guilty of the "upsell"?

Perhaps we have our own brand of the "Upsell." How many unnecessary MRI's, CT scans, lab tests, etc. do we order? And, even more importantly, why do we order them? And let me confess to you.

I, too, have succumbed to practicing the "upsell." I, too, have sometimes become the physician equivalent of Service Rep Bob. Let me share with you some of the reasons:

Fear: Medical legal issues. CYA.

Training: Medical school and residency trained me that I must consider every possibility and I must do every possible test to check out those possibilities.

Caution: I might miss some zebra diagnosis.

Hubris: Exotic and obscure tests that I order will reveal my neurological brilliance.

Paranoia: If I don't order tests, other physicians may criticize my lack of "adequate" workup.

Obsessive personality: I must find the answer to everything and find it now!

Patient feedback scores on my practice: If I don't order the tests that my patients request or demand, my patient feedback scores will suffer, or worse, my chief may get a patient complaint letter.

Mount Everest syndrome: Why'd you climb it?
"Because it was there!"
Why'd you order serum porcelain?
"Ditto."

Think about the downsides of ordering these unnecessary tests to us physicians:

- The time it takes to put in the orders.
- The time it takes to explain incidental findings (like a bulging disc on lumbar MRI).
- The clutter of our inboxes with superfluous lab and X-ray results.
- The unnecessary referrals they may engender, thus affecting specialist access.
- The extra work for other physicians, like radiologists, who must triage our requests.

- And perhaps, worst of all, the gut punch to our integrity as we find ourselves ordering tests we don't believe in.

And what about the risks of all this to our patients? (Not to mention the financial burden to the health care system.) Such as among other things:

- The co-pays working folks spend for these various X-rays and other tests.
- The time a patient must spend away from family and work for these tests.
- The worry and anxiety these tests put on patients and their families.
- The risk of radiation.
- The risk of the incidentaloma that leads to a harmful invasive procedure.

And, of course, when we explain why we are ordering a "serum porcelain" level to our patients, they may be just as in the dark as when Service Rep Bob suggests we need a manifold inspection. Yet our patients, too, may give the pseudo-knowing nod, sheepishly assenting to their doctor's "new and improved" service plan.

But for our patients, unlike with Service Rep Bob, the "upsell" is not about ginning up the maintenance of an automobile.

For our patients the "upsell" could put at risk their very lives.

What I'm saying is simply this:

Next time we are about to order that who-woulda-thunk-it test...let's think about Service Rep Bob. Let's think about why we are ordering the medical equivalent of that "transmission flush." And let's think about the potential consequences to our patients.

Addendum: Nowadays upon the advice of my service manager patient (who wishes to remain anonymous), my wife now hands Service Rep Bob a placard whenever she brings our car in for the routine service checkup. In big letters the note says: "NO UPSELL."

Perhaps when our "customers" come to our medical clinics for their routine service checkups, they should bring us a similar note.

TIME MANAGEMENT

TIME: THE BAD NEWS AND THE GOOD NEWS

Once upon a time back in the olden days, long, long ago, before there was such a thing as Hospital Based Specialists (HBS), all doctors rounded on their own hospitalized patients. Because clinic began at 8:30 a.m., most of us would start rounding on our hospitalized patients at about 7:00 a.m. It was always a tough-time challenge. Seeing these four or five hospitalized patients in this short-time window was difficult. I will admit, almost as I entered the room of patient number one, I'd be planning my exit strategy. I'd be thinking of how to expedite visits with patient number two, three, and four. I'd be time-panicked for the arrival of my 8:30 a.m. clinic patient. Frankly as I look back on those years, I know, as I made my morning rounds, I was not the most relaxed, focused, or compassionate physician.

That is why I marveled at my oncology colleague, Dr. Michael Jensen-Akula. He had the same patient load as everyone else, yet he always seemed calmly in control. And I marveled even more because his patients, unlike mine who could often be semi-comatose, would usually be alert, awake, and full of questions.

"Mike," I once asked, "how do you manage this? How do you make it through morning hospital rounds on patients so sick, so fearful, with so many questions, and with such brief time? What's the secret?"

"When I walk into my patient's room," answered Michael, "I make myself a promise. I vow to myself to spend ten totally dedicated minutes with that patient. And during that ten minutes there will be only two people on the planet: myself and my patient. I don't answer the beeper. I don't answer phone calls. My patient, in that sacred ten minutes, is my total focus. If Mother Teresa were giving birth to quintuplets in the next room, I would not budge."

I think I heard a wise man say this. (Or maybe I got it off the internet…they may be one and the same anyway.) But here's the teaching:

"The bad news: time flies. The good news: you can be the pilot."

And for this pilot's lesson, thank you, Dr. Michael Jensen-Akula.

COACH VINCE LOMBARDI WOULD LIKE THIS KAISER DOC

Dr. Alan Jung is an internal medicine physician in our Kaiser Union City facility.

The night before his upcoming appointments, Dr. Jung reviews the medical records of all his patients. He reviews the X-rays, the blood tests, and prior medical clinic appointments. He makes a note of any recent emergency room visits or any hospital admissions. He reminds himself of all the social activities and hobbies of his patients. This doctor works hard to prepare for his patients. Needless to say, his patients are impressed by his knowledge of their medical conditions. Needless to say his patients are impressed by his familiarity with their personal lives.

Vince Lombardi, the legendary coach of the Green Bay Packers, once said, "The most important thing is *not* the will to win. That is not what is crucial. Everyone who gets in a fight, everyone who competes, has the will to win."

"The most important thing," said Lombardi, "is the will to *prepare to win.*"

Coach Vince Lombardi would like Dr. Alan Jung.

TEAMWORK

WHY MY SON'S DOCTOR IS TOPS IN HIS FIELD

When my son Jeremy was seven years old, my wife took him to see the ear doctor. When I got home that night, I asked her how the visit went.

"Oh, everything went fine. That doctor," said Pamela, "is 'tops in his field.'"

I was curious. I am interested in that communication—bedside manner stuff. So I asked my wife how she came to that conclusion.

"Well," she answered (sounding annoyed that I could be so clueless as to ask such a silly question), "the nurse who put Jeremy in the exam room told me so!"

Wow!

Consider the teamwork between that nurse and her doctor.

If all of us had such teamwork, perhaps we all could be "tops in our field."

HOW SPECIALTY CONSULTANTS ARE LIKE MOTHERS

One day my wife greeted me with the dreaded ultimatum, "You better have a talk with that son of '*yours*.'" Did you catch that? Jeremy was now *my* son, not *hers*. Despite her genetic linkage Pamela had now abdicated all claims to his parentage. Jeremy, ten years old, had gotten into some trouble at Sunday school. The Sunday school teacher instructed the students to list nine Jewish prophets in the Bible.

Jeremy wrote in the starting lineup of the Oakland A's.

I tell this story because it reminds me of what an internal medicine doctor once told me.

"Why do my specialty consultants always report back that they saw *my* patient? Just once," she said, "couldn't they say the patient was *ours*?"

"GOOD MORNING AND THANK YOU"

Years ago, during the dark ages of labor management relations, our hospital had a labor dispute in which several unions went on strike. For several weeks our doctors filled in as hospital employees, doing everything from filling out admission forms of hospitalized patients to cleaning toilets. During one of my shifts, I worked as an assistant nurse. It was kind of weird but, after a while, not only did I perform my nursely duties, but I actually began to think like a nurse. I began to feel like a nurse.

Once I had trouble (surprise, surprise) reading a doctor's orders. (These were the days of preelectronic records.) I was told to page the doctor to clarify those particular orders.

Omigosh, I thought. *I didn't want to bother "my" doctor.*

What if he got annoyed at me?

What if he got angry?

Another time I remember reading the written orders of a certain surgeon.

The doctor began the orders with the words "Good morning."

He ended them with the words "Thank you."

Now it may seem like a trivial thing, but I can tell you, feeling like the beleaguered nurse I had become, these words really made me feel good. It was as if the doctor meant those comments especially for me. Later on I asked a nurse supervisor about this.

"Oh, yes," she replied, "Dr. Louis Ivey always writes his orders that way."

It's funny. Many years later I can still remember that incident. And I still remember how those simple polite words made me feel. Thank you, Dr. Louis Ivey.

HAVE YOU HUGGED YOUR CLEANING LADY TODAY?

Many years ago, I had a pinched nerve of my arm. Dr. Jay Whaley, a neurological colleague at Kaiser Permanente Redwood City, treated me. Jay sent me for X-rays. The radiology clerk looked at the X-ray request slip and then glanced up at me.

"Oh, Dr. Whaley is your doctor." She smiled. "He is such a nice man."

Now, of course, I knew that. But the fact that this radiology clerk gave Dr. Whaley this unsolicited endorsement was even more for me who knew and trusted Jay, a comforting reassurance. But it got me thinking. What if I were not Dr. Whaley's colleague; what if I were just your average apprehensive Joe Kaiser patient?

Imagine how reassuring those words from that clerk would have been then. And what if this same clerk, upon seeing Dr. Whaley's name, had rolled her eyes, or worse, made a negative comment? Perhaps ol' Joe Kaiser might have slithered straight out of the radiology suite.

This brings me to a recent report I heard from Johns Hopkins Medical School. Even if it's some sort of internet fable, it doesn't really matter. The truth is the same. Here's the story: A professor at that distinguished institution gave his medical students a ten-question pop quiz. The first nine questions dealt with usual medical stuff, like what bug causes what disease. The tenth question was, "What is the name of the cleaning lady in this building?"

Needless to say, none of the medical students got this question right; none scored 100 percent on the exam. They were miffed. So they did what any miffed medical student would do. They griped.

"Why did you ask that question," they moaned. "What has that got to do with medicine?"

"The answer to that question," the professor replied, "has everything to do with medicine."

Now I realize that a cleaning lady is not a radiology clerk.

But you get the connection.

Both have extraordinary power to affect the confidence folks have in their health care providers.

And now ask yourself this question: Have you hugged your cleaning lady today? (Okay, forget about the hugs.) Do you know her name?

WELLNESS AND RESILIENCE

HOW A "NOTHINGOMA" CAN BRING JOY TO PHYSICIANS

Joanne is a thirty-eight-year-old housewife and mother of four: two teens and twin girls, age ten. She was referred to me in neurology clinic because a routine brain MRI showed an abnormality. I talked with Joanne and examined her. Everything was perfectly fine. I reviewed the MRI. It clearly showed an incidental, harmless finding, a "Nothingoma," as we call it in the business. As I reassured her and was making my exit, Joanne grasped my hand between hers.

"Oh, Doctor," she tearfully exclaimed, "thank you so much. I was so worried. I am so grateful to you. God, bless you, Doctor."

To be honest I was embarrassed by this effusive praise. All I did was review a routine MRI. "Joanne," I rather sheepishly replied. "No problem. It was nothing."

But later that evening as I thought about the encounter, I realized this:

To Joanne this was a *SOMETHING*.

To Joanne this was a *BIG SOMETHING*.

And this should have been to me, a *SOMETHING*.

This should have been to me, a *BIG SOMETHING*.

I should have cherished that moment as much as she.

I saw a bumper sticker a while ago. It read: "It's amazing how you can affect someone's life so deeply and never appreciate it."

I will confess. For much of my medical career, I have been in the category of "never appreciate it." But I now understand. For Joanne, that encounter was a life-affirming blessing. And I now understand

173

that, for me, that encounter should have been just as much, such a blessing.

And to all my physician and healer colleagues, let me ask this question: How many of us are in the category of "never appreciate it"? How many of us ignore the blessings of our every day "Nothingomas"?

FOR PEACE OF MIND, RESIGN FROM THIS JOB

Janice seems to have what many of us in the medical profession euphemistically call "worried-well symptoms." For years I have tried to reassure her that her various episodes of tingling, dizziness, and body gurgles were nothing serious. Though Janice worries about everything she is actually a pretty normal housewife and mother. Awhile back she left me a message reporting her improvement.

"It's been two weeks now, Doc," she wrote, "and I'm still doing pretty good in your 'worried-well' recovery program. I haven't been on the internet once checking out the diseases that could afflict me and leave my children motherless."

We were both proud of her progress. On her next visit a few weeks later, she mentioned she was "relaxing" by attending her daughter's softball games.

"I sit in the stands," she continued, "to make sure my daughter doesn't get hit by a baseball."

I asked the obvious question.

"How could sitting in the stands prevent her daughter from getting hit by a ball?"

Janice had no answer.

As physicians and healers, I wonder, with our own patients (and our own loved ones), how many of us sit in the stands trying to make sure they don't get hit by a baseball?

Sometimes bad stuff will happen.

Sometimes we are powerless to prevent bad stuff from happening.

Sometimes we just can't fix bad stuff after it does happen.

Sometimes all we can do is hold the hands of those on their journey south.

"For peace of mind," a wise man once said, "resign as general manager of the universe."

WHERE DOES GOD DWELL?

"How many lives did you save today, Dad!"

That is what my kids would ask me, rather sarcastically, many years ago when they were young and when I arrived home late, missing our game of backyard basketball.

Now fast forward about thirty years. I saw Eleanor, an eighty-six-year-old woman in my neurology clinic. She had a common neurological diagnosis what we in the business call "Little Old Lady Dizziness." Of course there was nothing at all seriously wrong. But during the visit Eleanor told me her story.

Her husband had died nine months earlier. They had met roller skating. She thought he was the cutest guy in the roller rink. They were both nineteen. And for the next sixty-seven years they "skated" together. He was her husband, her lover, her best friend, her square dance partner, and her RV camping buddy.

As she told me the story Eleanor had a good cry. She had a good laugh. And though Eleanor was just as dizzy when she left my office as when she entered it, I felt good about the visit. I drove home that evening feeling a glow of satisfaction. On that day, I felt I had connected with my patient. On that day, I felt I had done something worthwhile.

And I had this thought: Had my sons greeted me this night with their usual sarcastic refrain, "How many lives did you save today, Dad?" Now, after this encounter with Eleanor, I would have replied differently.

"Fellas," I would have replied, "I did save a life today. I saw Eleanor. I heard her love story. I heard her grief story. I know she felt good talking to me. I know I felt good listening to her."

But the life I saved was not Eleanor's. On that day, in that encounter, I had allowed "joy and meaning in medicine" to bless my own life.

So what does this have to do with the question of "Where does God dwell?"

There is a teaching in the Hebrew Bible. A Rabbi asks his students that very question: "Where does God dwell?"

One student answered, "Heaven."

Another answered, "We are only human; we cannot possibly know where God dwells."

"No," the Rabbi replied. "God dwells wherever we choose to let God in."

Perhaps the same question could be asked about "joy and meaning in medicine."

Where does it dwell? And the answer may be the same. It dwells wherever we choose to let "joy and meaning in medicine" into our physician-healer lives.

As I look back upon my career, it saddens me to know that so often those doors to my dwelling were closed shut. For so often I had not a clue as to where lay the key to unlock them. For so many years this encounter would have been chalked up to another annoying, unfathomable "little old lady dizziness syndrome." But on that day, in that encounter, I was graced to have those doors opened by an eighty-six-year-old, dizzy, square-dancing roller skater.

I hope the doors of that dwelling never close again.

"THE BEST PHYSICIANS ARE DESTINED TO HELL"

This is a famous teaching of the Mishna, which in the Jewish faith is the commentary on the Torah, our Bible. Now why would the Holy Book of the Jews (of all people) make such a statement? Well, it turns out as my Rabbi explained, this is about arrogance. And it is about humility. The "best" doctors as we all know may also be the most prideful. They may not realize they need help. And if they do realize it, their macho self-assurance may prevent them from asking. And for this they may fail their patients.

I think there is some truth in this. I think most of us have had moments where in our professional lives, we have not reached out to colleagues because of fear of looking stupid or of feeling incompetent. Of this I know I have been guilty. Mea culpa.

But this teaching may be true in another way. Sometimes when we, "the best physicians," are suffering from emotional exhaustion and staring burnout in its charred face, we ourselves don't reach out. We don't ask for help. For many of us the story of our professional lives is this: We face overwhelming workloads, long hours in the hospital, and even more hours at home with our hospital-issued portable computer (my "laptop lover," my wife, Pamela, calls it).

We spend countless, frustrating hours doing clerical work that a medical secretary could do. We cancel dinner dates with spouses and friends. We miss our kids' soccer games and music recitals. But in the face of this overwhelming pressure, what do we do? How do we respond? Most of us do what we always have done. We put our heads down and work harder. We plow through. We suck it up. We tough it out because "when the going gets tough..." (you can fill in the blank).

We are made of grit, backbone, pluck, and spunk. We are not quitters. We bite the bullet, swallow the pill, pay the piper. We do all this, but we don't ask for help. We persevere in silence. And while we may tough it out, our flame gets dimmer. We see (or maybe we don't see) the beginnings of burnout.

So if there is a kernel of truth in all this for anyone, please reach out to someone: a trusted colleague, a loved one, a Physician Well-being committee member, the Employee Assistance program, a psychiatrist, a counselor in your faith community, *someone*.

Maybe the "best physicians" are "destined to hell." But if you, my physician brothers and sisters, feel like you are headed toward this destination, please heed this warning:

Do not take this journey alone.

And if you see your fellow physician brothers and sisters heading down this path, think about lending a helping hand, a warm shoulder, or a listening ear.

Remember: friends do not let friends become "the best doctors."

"IF GOD WANTED YOU TO BE PERFECT..."

I realized I had made a mistake caring for a patient. As I sat on Ward 2 West, no doubt looking very anguished, Dr. Norman Walter, a veteran surgeon, must have noticed my doleful expression. I explained to him the situation and how I had overlooked something important in the care of my patient.

"Listen, buddy boy," said Dr. Walter as he pinched, then jiggled my cheeks. "if the good Lord wanted you to be perfect, He would have created you into a CAT scan machine!"

I think back on this from time to time.

I have learned some new ways to look at it.

"Striving for excellence," a famous psychologist once said, "motivates you. Striving for perfection is demoralizing."

Or in the words of my grandmother, "No one is perfect...that's why pencils have erasers."

THIS THOUGHT NEVER OCCURRED TO ME

A student nurse in our hospital approached me. She was curious about a neurology patient. After discussing the particular patient, she then told me the best part of her week was when she was out of the classroom and had the opportunity to work on the wards with patients.

"At the end of each shift," she said, "I visit each of my patients to thank them personally for the privilege of taking care of them."

It's funny.

As a physician, I've been doing this job for over forty years.

The thought of doing that never occurred to me.

SAVOR THAT COCA-COLA

Douglas Boakye, a physician in our San Leandro-Fremont hospital, grew up in a tiny village in Ghana, West Africa. In those days, Dr. Boakye recalls, the biggest treat in his life occurred once a year at Christmas time.

On this day twelve months of yearning were finally fulfilled.

On this day he was given the yearly prize of his young life:

On this day Douglass Boakye was given a Coca-Cola!

(Actually he was given only about one quarter of a glass, not even a full coke, but that did not diminish the ecstasy of the day.)

Nowadays, of course, Dr. Boakye can have a full glass of Coca-Cola anytime he wants. Yet Douglass has not forgotten his days as a child in that small, poor West African village.

"America is a wonderful place. I appreciate everything I have," says Dr. Boakye. "And I still savor every sip of every Coca-Cola I ever drink."

Here is a question:

How many of us savor every sip of our Coca-Colas?

"ME TIME"

Dr. Mayura Suryanara transferred from working full-time in the hospital to working full-time in the outpatient clinic. I asked if life was any easier for her in the outpatient clinic; I asked if she had more time with her family nowadays. Mayura said the hours worked out about the same, but in the clinic, work was predictable: it was 8:00 a.m. to 5:00 p.m. (ha ha), but she knew she had evenings and weekends off.

She was now available to do family stuff with her kids and her husband. On the other hand, even though she worked about the same amount of hours as a hospital doctor, hospital shift schedules were unpredictable. Mayura often had had stretches of Tuesdays and Wednesdays off work when kids were at school and husband at work.

"I love my family," Mayura smiled, "but, truth be told, I do miss those Tuesday and Wednesdays off. I miss those coffee shop mornings. I miss the lazy reading of the morning newspaper. I miss those days that I had all to myself. I miss the '*me*' time."

Memo to physicians and healers:

"Don't we all need some '*me*' time?"

ALMOST

There is an old story.

A man is at the funeral of his wife.

Filled with tears he tells the preacher, "I loved my wife."

The preacher nods his head.

"No," the man cries out, "I really loved her!"

"I understand," says the preacher.

"And one time," wails the grief-racked husband, "I *almost* told her."

As physicians and healers, as we speed through our hectic, multitasking lives, let's hope that with our own loved ones, we never regret the "*almost.*"

I AM THANKFUL I AM MISERABLE

Driving to work one morning, I got stuck helplessly for two hours in a bad traffic jam on the San Mateo-Hayward Bridge.

My beeper was beeping.

My cell phone was ringing.

My patients were angry.

My staff was frustrated.

I was getting pretty cranky myself.

Finally, I got to work.

My first patient was a woman of thirty-three with two young children.

She had multiple sclerosis.

She was in a wheelchair.

She would be in one for the rest of her life.

Woody Allen once said: "Life is divided into the horrible and the miserable."

"The horrible," he said, "is like a tornado in Oklahoma or like starvation in Africa."

Or, I suppose, like a mother who will never walk.

"The miserable," said Woody, "is everything else."

Looking back on that woeful traffic jam morning, I try to remind myself to be thankful for the "everything else."

I try to remind myself to be thankful for woeful traffic jams.

I try to remind myself, as Woody Allen says, to be thankful for the miserable.

WORK-LIFE BALANCE

WORK-LIFE BALANCE... BACKWARDS WHY WE MIGHT OBSESS OVER BORDERLINE CHLORIDE LEVELS

When we talk about "work-life balance," what we often imply is that our devotion to our work life is so overwhelming and out of balance that we sacrifice time with our families. So we struggle to limit our work time in order to make more home time.

I wonder if this sometimes works the other way too. I wonder if when homelife is not working out too well and its problems sometimes are overwhelming to us that we end up spending more time at work, that we turn to our work for support and comfort.

I will confess:

During the forty years I spent as a physician, I experienced this very thing firsthand. I had some rocky stretches with homelife, marriage, and kids. For example, when my sons were teenagers, they had (let's use the euphemistic phrase) "issues." I won't go into details, but I'll repeat. They had "issues."

There were many times that I actually looked forward to weekend call. And on regular workdays arriving at my office (as early as possible), the musical sound of the awakening of my computer's electronic record seemed a sweet melody indeed. In those difficult days, before going home, I would search for more clinic stuff to do: one last check of the inbox, a patient phone call to make, or a lab test to follow-up on, all to delay my arrival home, a home where I hoped the family crisis du jour would blow over by the time I arrived (or at least my wife, not me, would bear the brunt of the storm). As hectic as work might be, at least at work I had some control. At least there I received some respect. And in those dark days, while in my home, I did not perceive myself experiencing either control or respect.

Of course the good news, thankfully, for me and my family is that all those issues with kids and marriage and life have worked out in the long run. In spite of those rocky times in the past I consider my life to have been truly blessed.

So why do I write this now?

I want to share with you, my colleagues, that if you are going through the same thing: if you repeatedly open your inbox for the "last" time before you leave work, if you linger over borderline lab work before heading home, or if you find that the melody of your computer's electronic record as it turns on…well…also "turns you on," so to speak, then…

You are not alone. You've got company. It happened with me.

My dear colleagues:

May your work-home balance soon turnaround the right way. And may you no longer linger at work pondering those borderline chloride levels.

THE "C" GAME

"By the time I'm done seeing patients," said Dr. Sung Choe, my ophthalmologist colleague, "finishing my charting, tidying up my in-basket, making the callbacks to worried folks, filling out disability forms and jury excuse letters, and then rushing off to pick up my daughter before the day care deadline, I'm exhausted. I'm just spent. Lots of times I don't even have the energy to read my daughter a bedtime story. Lots of nights I don't even have the energy to have a conversation with my wife. And sometimes I snap at them both over nothing.

"It's crazy: My patients get my 'A' game. My wife and daughter get my 'C' game. I don't have the answers to these challenges. But I do know this: We are not alone. We all struggle to find balance between our personal and our professional lives. We are all disheartened when we cannot give both our patients and our families the 'A' game. And just for the record...

"In spite of everything," Dr. Choe concluded, "I would still choose to be a physician."

I bet most of us would too. And therein lies the challenge. Let me close with questions posed by social commentator Dennis Prager:

Whatever one does for a living, three questions need to be confronted before it is too late.

What really matters to me?

What price do my spouse and my kids pay for my career success?

What price does my soul pay?

And maybe there is an answer after all.

At least the first step to one.

Because the first step to finding an answer...is to ask the questions.

"THE QUESTION"

On hospital call duty for neurology, I had a particularly intense and hectic three nights. I didn't get home till maybe 9:00 p.m. or 10:00 p.m. each night. When I finally got home Sunday night, my wife hit me with *the question*: "Who do you love better," Pamela demanded, "your patients or me?"

Now I am no dummy. I responded immediately, "It is you, my beautiful bride, that I love the most."

"I don't believe you," Pamela uttered as she turned and walked away. That night my sleep home was the guest bedroom.

However, with some Ghirardelli Chocolates and with some apologetic sweet-talkin', by the next night I was back in our master bedroom. And of course Pamela is no stranger to these kind of work weekends. She knew this when she married into the medical profession forty-one years ago. But sometimes, I guess, it still gets to her.

I suspect that many doctors have, at one time or another, been on the receiving end of the "Who do you love better?" question.

Now it is one thing when one's spouse or partner asks *the question*.

But what about when our kids ask?

And what may be even more disheartening is when they don't ask.

What if they silently presume the answer?

"I GAVE AT THE OFFICE"

Debra Matityahu, a busy OB-GYN doctor in Redwood City, Kaiser, told me that far too often when her husband has had a bad day and when he is looking for a little TLC, she has found herself snapping at him.

"Look, honey," said Debbie, "so you had a tough day. I get it. But I just can't feel a lot of empathy for you tonight. I gave at the office!"

WHY MY WIFE (ALMOST) WISHED SHE HAD A NEUROLOGICAL DISEASE

My wife has been a housewife and mother the forty-three years of our marriage. But there were times in the past when Pamela said she almost wished she had some unusual neurological disease; there were times in the past when she said she fantasized about being one of my patients.

"At least then," Pamela chided me, "I might get some attention!"

"HONEY, YOU NEED TO TAKE CARE OF YOUR WIFE!"

Dr. Jerald Wisdom, an ophthalmologist in San Jose Kaiser, says that during a clinic day, he sometimes gets "Howdy" calls from his wife. Dr. Wisdom admitted that one time to end this wifely social chat, he said something like: "Honey, I need to go. I need to take care of my electronic medical record."

"Honey," his wife responded, "tell your electronic medical record…you need to take care of your wife!"

I live in San Mateo, California, the heart of the Silicon Valley high-tech industry. A while ago I saw in my neighborhood a bumper sticker. It read: "Husbands, love your wives just as you love your smartphone."

Maybe the same advice is good for us physicians.

Maybe we need to show expression of love to our wives as much as to our electronic medical record mistresses.

Addendum: As is my custom, I always run these monthly columns by my own wife to get her opinion. She said this was the best one I ever wrote.

PLAYGROUND LAPTOPS

Walking through a children's playground, I saw two kids giggling excitedly as they played on the monkey bars. On a nearby bench, Dad, a spiffy, professional-looking guy, was busily inputting on his laptop.

It was a sunny day.

The children were laughing.

Yet laptop Dad seemed oblivious to all this.

Here is what I wonder: When we go to the playground with our own kids, how often do we bring with us our own laptops? Either the tangible ones we place on our laps or the invisible ones whose open browser tabs clog our minds to the joy, laughter, and beauty all around us?

"I WISH I WOULD HAVE SPENT MORE TIME..."

Have you heard the old joke?

An old guy is lying on his deathbed.

Family and loved ones are all around him.

The old guy looks over the gathering.

"Doggone," he says, "I wish I would have spent more time in my business."

I thought this was kind of funny.

It's funny because no one really says stuff like that.

But for us physicians and healers, what is unfunny is that though we don't say stuff like that, sometimes we live it. Sometimes we live it every day.

Sometimes (and Lord knows, in this regard, I am a big-time sinner), we live our hectic, multitasking, professional lives as if with our last dying breath, we, too, might whisper something like "Doggone, I wish I would have treated just one more urinary tract infection. Boy, oh boy, then my life would have been so complete!"

"YOU KNOW"

Hank was one of toughest old birds I've ever encountered as a patient. He had to be. In his twenties, he was in a terrible motorcycle accident which horrifically scarred and deformed his face. Hank seemed to delight in giving everyone a hard time, especially his Kaiser doctors. He would announce to a room full of astonished folks in our clinic waiting area: "Can you believe it? Abramson's working today! Golf game musta got canceled." (Personal note: I have never golfed in my life.)

He called me, "Dr. No."

"Abramson," he chortled, "You 'no' nothing. You do nothing. You tell me nothing."

His wife once told me this story: their only son, even as a grown man, would plead with his father, "Just say the words, dad. For once, tell me you love me."

Hank always answered the same way.

"You know," he grumbled. "You know."

So ol' Hank died a month ago. On his tombstone are engraved the words "You Know."

All this got me thinking.

Sometimes those who love us need to hear more than the words "You know."

WHY I FELT GOOD ABOUT TAKING MY MISTRESS ON VACATION

I went on vacation with my wife to Hawaii.

I took my mistress with us.

(That is how my wife refers to my Kaiser-issued laptop.)

Every day on the beautiful isle of Maui, I logged on to my hospital's laptop electronic medical record system.

Even on vacation, I would be able to take care of my practice.

I felt good about this.

Here's why:

1. I would be able to avoid the "back from vacation" deluge of messages.
2. I would make things easier on my colleagues who would be covering my practice.
3. And of course, I could take care of some of my patients' needs in my "absence."

But there is another reason why I felt good about this.

I'm not particularly proud of this.

My wife says I'm a sick puppy.

Okay.

Here goes.

I confess.

I feel a little guilty when I take vacation.

A voice within is whispering.

It tells me I shouldn't be doing nothing!

It tells me I should be doing something…something useful!

It tells me I should not be lazing around on the beach, drinking some pretty concoction with a fake little wooden umbrella in it.

While this may be an unnatural affliction (as my wife reminds me), yet still, somehow, I continue to feel good about taking my laptop on vacation.

I know it is deeply pathological.

But I wonder:

Is anyone out there with a similar affliction?

Anyone want to join me in a support group?

Consider this outreach to all Laptop Lunatics.

(And yes, I am HIPPA compliant.)

Addendum: The Laptop Lunatic support group meets only on weekends and holidays.

(And, of course, bring your mistress.)

THE SECRET OF
HAPPINESS

THE SECRET OF HAPPINESS

I have learned the secret of happiness.

This, of course, is good news for me.

But for those who are reading this piece, it is even better news. Because being the prince of a fellow that I am, I shall share with you this incredible wisdom. But first let me explain how I came upon this epiphany.

Every day I drove to work from San Mateo to Hayward across the nine-mile San Mateo-Hayward Bridge. Usually it was a pretty good commute. But since the San Mateo-Hayward Bridge in those days was a bridge without exit ramps or shoulder lanes over a bay of water, when an accident occurred, the commute would be tied up for hours. This is exactly what happened on a fateful day several years ago. Bad accident. A busy clinic was awaiting me that morning and I was stuck on the freakin' bridge going nowhere. Inside my car, I howled with helpless fury at the gods of bridge traffic. I began to commit aggressive acts upon my steering wheel. Adjacent motorists deliberately avoided looking my way. Finally, about three hours later still fuming with frustration, I arrived at work.

As I parked my car in the hospital lot, I happened to see Consuelo who travels the same bridge commute. Consuelo was our clinic's Environmental Service Technician (translation: garbage person). Consuelo, amazing to behold, was her usual pleasant, even-tempered, and yes, happy self. I couldn't believe it.

"Consuelo," I demanded, "you were stalled on the bridge for the last three hours just like me. Why aren't you seething with resentment and rage like...like...a normal person! How come you look so doggone happy!"

And then Consuelo laid upon me this great wisdom.

She revealed to me the secret of happiness.

"Oh, Dr. Abramson," she smiled, "I am just so grateful. I am so grateful that I wasn't the one in the accident."

One annoying event.

Two human responses.

One is miserable.

One is happy.

Guess which one lives a life filled with gratitude?

And there you have it:

The secret of happiness is…attitude.

And the secret of attitude is…gratitude.

ABOUT THE AUTHOR

Scott Abramson, MD, for over forty years, enjoyed a rewarding career as a neurologist at the Kaiser Permanente Medical Group in the San Francisco Bay Area.

For most of his career Dr. Abramson has been passionately involved in the Kaiser communication mission (teaching bedside manners to physicians). During this time Dr. Abramson has developed programs on time management, physician communication, marriage in medicine, burnout, the threatened physician, difficult conversations, storytelling, and his two favorites, "The Secret of Happiness" and "The Great Wisdom in Country Music Speaks to our Physician Lives."

In 1982 Dr. Abramson was awarded the Physician of the Year honor in his medical facility. In 2003 he was given Teaching Excellence Award from Physician Education, and in 2010 was nominated as a Kaiser Hero for his work in regional physician communication.

On a personal note, Dr. Abramson has been a longtime volunteer at the Samaritan House Medical Clinic in San Mateo, California, helping provide medical care for the indigent of that county. He has also been in years past a longtime volunteer at the USO, helping to provide rest and respite to the young men and women in our armed forces. Currently he is also a volunteer with the MAVEN project, an organization of retired physicians who offer their consultative services to clinics in underserved areas all over America.

Dr. Abramson lives with his wife, Pamela, of forty-four years in San Mateo, California. They have two sons, Jonathan, living in

Spokane, Washington, and Jeremy who is a personal development coach. (Check him out on Instagram: @coachjeremy305.)

Dr. Abramson has set foot in forty-eight of fifty states, lacking only Wisconsin and North Dakota. He and his sons have attended baseball games in twenty-six major league stadiums. (And they proudly boast that in all those games, no Abramson family member has ever participated in the wave!)

Retired from his Kaiser Permanente medical career in 2020, nowadays Dr. Abramson and his wife take daily walks on the beaches of Half Moon Bay, California, where they enjoy their new life mission: *garbage collection* (garbage grabber $19.98 at Home Depot).

abramsonbedsidemanners@gmail.com

Printed in the USA
CPSIA information can be obtained
at www.ICGtesting.com
LVHW041050061023
760263LV00033B/379